saving maddie

saving maddie

VARIAN JOHNSON

DELACORTE PRESS

Copyright © 2010 by Varian Johnson

All rights reserved. Published in the United States by Delacorte Press, an imprint of Random House Children's Books, a division of Random House, Inc., New York.

Delacorte Press is a registered trademark and the colophon is a trademark of Random House, Inc.

Visit us on the Web! www.randomhouse.com/teens

Educators and librarians, for a variety of teaching tools, visit us at www.randomhouse.com/teachers

Library of Congress Cataloging-in-Publication Data is available upon request.
ISBN 978-0-385-73804-0 (hardcover)
ISBN 978-0-385-96708-8 (lib. bdg.)
ISBN 978-0-375-89592-0 (e-book)

The text of this book is set in 12.5-point Eidetic Neo Regular.

Book design by Angela Carlino

Printed in the United States of America
10 9 8 7 6 5 4 3 2 1

First Edition

To the Quills, with love

ACKNOWLEDGMENTS

I would like to thank my friends, classmates, and advisors at the Vermont College of Fine Arts, especially Sharon Darrow and Rita Williams-Garcia, as this novel would not be what it is today without your guidance. Thanks to my editor, Stephanie Lane Elliott; editorial assistant Krista Vitola; and my agent, Sara Crowe, for your tireless work and dedication. Thanks to Helen Hemphill, Frances Hill, Julie Lake, April Lurie, Brian Yansky, and Cynthia Leitich Smith for your advice, support, and friendship.

And always, thanks to my wife and family for letting me do what I was born to do.

In the Beginning
(Five Years Ago)

"Hurry up," she yelled, dust blowing in her wake as she ran down the dirt trail. "You're slower than a three-legged dog."

I did my best to keep up, but even in her long yellow dress and slip-on shoes, Maddie Smith was easily outpacing me—just like always. Of course, she didn't pay any mind to her clothes, while I tried my best to keep my white button-down shirt clean. How would it look, us sneaking back into the church during the offering, our clothes looking like we'd crawled through a pigpen? Our mothers would have a fit, if they didn't die of embarrassment first.

Maddie stopped at an old, worn wooden fence at the end of the path. The trail continued as a gravel path to both her left and right, but Maddie didn't seem interested in going in either direction.

Red-hot flashes of pain raced up the sides of my body. "You sure we should be skipping out like this? Won't they notice we're gone?" I wanted to lean over and brace myself against the fence, but I wasn't about to be shown up by Maddie. She might have been my best friend, but she was still a girl.

"Since my daddy became assistant pastor, do you know how many church services I've missed?" She formed her hand into a zero. "I think God'll forgive me for skipping one little service."

"But your dad . . . I don't want you to get into trouble. . . ."

"How about you let me worry about that." Maddie placed her hands on the top rail and pushed herself over the fence. "Well? You coming or what?" she asked.

"That's Mrs. Watson's property."

"So?"

"We'd be trespassing. It's against the law."

Maddie jutted out her hip and crossed her arms. "Joshua Wynn! It's not like anyone's going to haul us off to jail."

"But—"

"I swear, if you don't get over here right now, I'm going to pick you up and toss you over."

I knew Maddie well enough to know she was telling the truth. Even though she was nothing but skin, knees, and elbows, she was unusually strong for a thirteen-year-old.

I took a running start and leapt over the fence. As soon as I landed, she started running again. "Now come on. It isn't much farther."

Maddie had promised to show me her secret hideaway—where she snuck off to when our parents were stuck in a meeting at church, or when she wanted to get away from her house, or when she was just plain bored. I guess she figured that since she'd be leaving in a couple of days, she might as well pass her secret place on to me.

I felt another pain in my chest, but I knew this didn't have anything to do with running. Now who was I supposed to joke with about how Mrs. Martin always sang off-key, or how Deacon Fisk always smelled like liquor? Who else was I going to hang out with when my father was stuck in a three-hour meeting at church? Who else's long brown legs was I going to stare at when I was supposed to be reading my Bible?

Maddie stopped at the edge of a thicket filled with lush green leaves and chocolate-brown tree branches. She grabbed my hand, even though it was hot and sweaty. "Watch your step. It's dark in here."

She led me out of the sunlight into the overgrown brush. We walked in silence, sidestepping decaying tree trunks and thorny shrubs, until we arrived at an old, decrepit shed surrounded by a huge blackberry bush.

I raced over to the bush, dropped to my knees, and plucked a handful of blackberries from the twisted, thorny stems. The blackberries were warm and soft, and I was afraid they were going to burst if I even touched them the wrong way.

Maddie crouched beside me. "I figured this would be better than any gift I could buy." She popped a few blackberries into her mouth, then showed me her purple tongue.

I laughed in between chewing. "Why didn't you tell me about this place earlier? You know how much I love blackberries."

Her smile faded. "Sometimes you need a place of your own, you know. Between my parents and my sisters, I can't ever get any peace and quiet at home. This is the only place where I can think."

I munched on another blackberry. "Well, you won't have to worry about that pretty soon. Your dad says that y'all's new house is even bigger than the one y'all have now." Maddie never mentioned it, but I heard enough gossip from the ladies at church to know that her mom had been born into money. "I hear y'all are getting a swimming pool and everything."

Maddie shrugged. "I don't even like to swim." She stood back up and crossed her arms, and I couldn't help but notice that her dress was getting a little snug around her chest. Maybe she wasn't *all* skin and bones.

A leaf floated from the sky and landed on her collar, right where her freckled skin met the edge of her yellow dress. She brushed the leaf away, but in the process smeared blackberry juice on her top.

I rose to my feet and pointed at the three purple blotches. "Your dress . . ."

Maddie looked down. "Shoot. This is the third dress I've messed up this year."

I reached for her. "Here, let me help–"

She swatted my hand away. "Joshua Wynn, I'm not about to stand here and let you cop a feel."

"I didn't mean—I wasn't going to . . ." I stumbled a few steps backward. "I was just trying to help."

She broke into a grin. "I'm joking, Joshua. Calm down." She stuck her thumb into her mouth, then tried to rub out the blackberry stain. "I know you'd never try to do something like that. You aren't like those stupid boys in my gym class. You know how to treat girls with respect."

Maybe *she* thought I was respectful, but the guys at school didn't see it that way. They said I was scared. Actually, they called me worse names than that, but according to my parents, good Christian boys like me weren't supposed to repeat such abominable words.

Even if I wasn't scared, it really didn't matter, because Maddie was a full year older than me, and it was common knowledge that girls didn't date down. Plus, she had been my best friend for as long as I could remember, and she'd think it was weird.

More importantly, it didn't matter how I felt about her because she was leaving for Virginia the day after tomorrow.

"I guess I'm going to be stuck with a blackberry stain on my dress." All Maddie had succeeded in doing was making the stain even bigger. Her thumb was dark from the blackberry juice.

I nodded toward her dress, careful not to focus too much on her chest. "Sorry."

"Don't worry about it; it'll just give my parents something new to complain about." She picked at her fingernails, trying to get out the blackberry juice. "So, you're not going to forget about me as soon as I leave, are you?"

"Of course not. I'll e-mail you every day."

"E-mail is so . . . impersonal. I like letters instead. You can tell so much about someone from the way they write their words. Plus, Dad won't let us get the Internet. He thinks the Web is a playground for the devil."

"Okay, then. We'll do letters." I would write her, e-mail her, telegram her—whatever she wanted.

Maddie stopped picking at her fingernails. "Come on. You know the drill."

I laughed. Then I spit on my palms, rubbed them together, and crossed my heart. "*I promise.* I'll write you. A lot."

Maddie spit in her own palm and repeated the pledge. "And I promise to write back." She looked down at her hands and laughed. "We're getting too old to be doing that, aren't we?"

I tried to memorize every freckle on her nose. "Some things never get old."

The wind picked up around us, pushing her scent toward me, and I took in a deep breath. The smell of her vanilla shampoo seemed right in place with the sweet taste of blackberry in my mouth.

Maddie tilted her head to the side, burrowing her big brown eyes into me. "I'm really going to miss this place," she said. "I'm really going to miss you."

I'd swear Maddie's eyes were big enough to swim in. There wasn't a lot of light filtering through the branches, but somehow just enough of the sun's rays hit her face, almost causing it to glow. This was the image of Maddie I wanted to remember—smiling and sweet and pure.

"Joshua . . ." Maddie stepped closer, moving a little out of the light. "There's something else I want to give you before I go." She took another step, and I lost her gaze in the shadows. "You ever kissed a girl before?"

My heart jumped up in my chest, and my knees buckled. "I . . . I . . ."

She smiled. "I don't even know why I asked. You'd have told me if you did. You tell me everything."

A surge of energy rushed through my veins. "Well, almost everything." I moved toward her.

Maddie placed her stained fingers on my white shirt. I couldn't have cared less if they left a mark. "Well . . ."

She closed her eyes and I closed mine. I took in her scent again—I didn't think I'd ever eat another scoop of vanilla ice cream without dreaming about her.

I started to lean in, but seconds before I was about to connect with her, I heard it.

Barking. Lots and lots of barking.

I flashed my eyes open and saw that Maddie was staring at me. Her eyebrows had furrowed into tight bunches on her forehead. "I can't believe—"

"What's going on over there?"

Maddie and I jumped away from each other. I kept my gaze glued to the ground as the sound of footsteps crunched toward us.

I looked back up to see Mrs. Watson planted a few feet away from us, her dogs howling at her feet. "Maddie Smith? Joshua?" She narrowed her eyes. "Shouldn't y'all be in church?"

I nodded, my neck stiff and tense.

The Labrador retrievers struggled to reach us, but Mrs. Watson kept a firm grip on the dogs' leashes. Huge veins snaked underneath her pale, thick arms. "Y'all know better than to sneak out here by yourselves," she said, her cheeks puffing as she spoke. "Think what kind of example y'all are setting for the rest of the children."

Maddie cleared her throat. "But we weren't—"

"I may be old, but I ain't blind. I know perfectly well what y'all were up to." She shook her head, causing her stringy white hair to cascade in front of her eyes. "There's no telling what y'all would have done if I hadn't caught y'all," she said. "With y'all's daddies being preachers and all, y'all should especially know better."

Maddie marched toward Mrs. Watson. "Now wait a minute. Just because—"

"We're sorry," I interrupted. I ran after Maddie, grabbed her hand, and pulled her away from Mrs. Watson and her killer dogs. "We're heading back to church now."

The dogs howled behind us. "Don't think this means I ain't gonna tell y'all's parents," she called out. She yelled something else, but her words got lost in the dogs' barks and yelps.

All the way back to the fence, I was too ashamed to look at Maddie. I just focused on putting one foot in front of the other, and prayed that my face wasn't turning colors.

Once we reached the fence, Maddie shook my hand loose. "That old cow!"

I looked at Maddie. Her cheeks were dark red, but I figured it was less from shame and more from anger.

I shrugged. "Well, we *were* trespassing."

Maddie snorted. "Listen, Joshua. Some rules are just plain stupid. Some rules shouldn't even be rules in the first place." She pulled her hair off her neck and twisted it into a bun. "And some rules . . . well, some rules are made to be broken."

I nodded like I understood what she was saying, even though she was making absolutely no sense. Rules weren't supposed to be broken. That was why they were called *rules.* And if you broke them, you had to deal with the repercussions of your actions. It was that simple. That was what the Bible said.

"What do you think your dad'll do to you?" I asked. I knew he could be pretty strict sometimes.

The skin around her eyes creased. "Don't know. I imagine I'll find out soon enough." Then she grinned, showing off that blackberry smile. "Come on. I'll race you back."

Not waiting for my response, she leapt over the fence and sprinted back to the church. I laughed and took off after her, even though I knew full well I was going to lose.

chapter 1

Ms. Regina Howard, our older-than-Moses choir director, had a set of rules we were all supposed to abide by on Sunday morning. Don't chew gum. Pay attention to the sermon. No talking. You know, the usual stuff.

Being the only son of the Reverend Isaiah P. Wynn, I was expected to never break the rules. Ever. Which was why I grew more and more irritated as Tony and the rest of the guys in the choir stand kept whispering to each other. Of course, I hadn't been included in the conversation, even though I was sitting smack dab in the middle of the group.

I tugged on Tony's robe. "Will y'all shut up? Y'all are going to get us in trouble."

"Sorry," Tony mumbled, although he didn't look at me. Something in the audience had captured his attention. Whatever it was, it was a lot more interesting than Dad's sermon. I tried to follow his gaze, but nothing or no one special in the congregation caught my eye.

As soon as the guys quieted down, I leaned closer to Tony. "So what were you looking at so hard?" I asked.

"Nothing," he said, his breath sweet with the scent of a green apple Jolly Rancher.

Tony turned toward my father and pretended to pay attention to the sermon, but truth be told, I wasn't even listening to Dad. To be fair, it was kind of hard to pay attention to something you had already heard the night before. I was Dad's soul-saving guinea pig.

"Come on, Tony," I whispered as Dad was about to launch into his final point. "Just tell me what y'all were looking at."

Tony sighed. "Weren't you just saying something about how I needed to shut up? Something about getting into trouble?"

"Tony . . ."

He grinned. "Fifth pew. Third one from the aisle," he said. "The hottie in the black dress."

Had he forgotten where we were? "Tony, I'm not about to–"

"Hey, you're the one that asked," he said. "Don't look if you don't want to. But she kind of looks like Jenn, from a distance."

My gaze raced past the first four pews. Past Delano

Jackson, in a striped shirt that looked three sizes too small. Past Mrs. Luretha Mae Madison, with her big white pillbox hat.

And then I saw her. But she wasn't my ex-girlfriend.

"I can't . . ." I blinked hard, just to make sure I wasn't making a mistake. "I can't believe . . ."

"Okay, so maybe she doesn't look like Jenn," Tony said. "Still, she looks good."

I would have nodded, but I was too busy staring at the girl.

No, not girl. *Woman.*

No, not Jenn. *Maddie.*

Tony nudged me. "You see what she's wearing? Any second now, I bet she's going to bust out of that dress."

I frowned. "Shut up."

"But—"

"I mean it, Tony. Shut up."

He scowled but kept his eyes on Maddie. I wanted to raise my Bible to his face to block his view. She didn't deserve to be gawked at.

Tony did have a point, though. Her dress was awfully formfitting. I didn't realize that she had become so . . . blessed. But then again, I hadn't seen her in over five years.

I turned back to Tony, who was still staring at her. I dug my elbow into his ribs, hard enough for his breathing to stop.

"Do you have to stare at her like that?" I asked.

He rubbed his side. "Don't blame me. Daniel's the one that started it."

I looked past Tony at the other guys in our row of the choir stand, each of their gazes locked onto Maddie. At least for today, the tenor section of the choir had conveniently chosen to ignore the tenth commandment.

Dad ground through his sermon, finally bringing it to a close in his usual thunderous fashion. The entire congregation leapt to their feet and clapped their hands in praise. Well, almost everyone. Maddie stayed firmly in her seat.

After all the announcements had been made and all the collection plates had been passed around, Dad proclaimed his final *amen*. Seconds later, Maddie marched toward the door.

I pried off my white choir robe and dumped it into Tony's hands. "Hold on to this for me. I'll be back in a few minutes."

"But what about the youth group meeting?"

"Tell Donna to start without me."

I made my way from the choir stand and sliced through the crowd. Like always, people kept jumping in front of me, wanting to stop and shoot the breeze. I tried to keep my eyes on Maddie but lost her in a sea of pastel-colored dresses and three-button suits.

I pushed my way out of the building. Compared to the glow of the crystal chandeliers in the sanctuary, it seemed almost dark outside. The warm summer air, mixed with the humidity from the previous night's downpour, reminded me of the swamps down at Congaree National Park.

I scanned the parking lot until I saw her, her gaze glued to the ground, her arms folded across her body. I didn't know people could move so quickly in high heels.

Ignoring the rain puddles, I hightailed it through the parking lot, mud splattering across my wingtips. I caught up with her just as she reached the edge of the lot.

"Maddie?"

She stopped and turned around. Her eyes narrowed for a second, then relaxed. "Joshua Wynn?" Her lips stretched into a smile. "I *thought* that was you up there in the choir."

I nodded. "What are you doing back in South Carolina?"

"It's a long story," she said as she enveloped me in a bear hug. "Let's just say I needed a break."

I wrapped my arms around her; my fingers froze for a half second as they grazed her bra strap. I took in her scent—her familiar vanilla practically hidden by a coffee smell. "I almost didn't recognize you," I said.

She pulled away. "I look that different, huh?"

Heat shot to my face. "Well . . . I didn't mean . . ."

"It's okay. I know I've changed a lot." She looked me up and down. "But then again, so have you."

My tie felt like a noose around my neck. "I must have finally put on a few pounds." I moved closer to her to allow people to pass by. "Wow. Maddie, I can't believe—"

"Call me Madeline. I go by my full name now."

"Madeline." I liked the way the word felt on my

tongue. "I guess that sounds a lot more mature than Maddie."

"Like I said before, I've changed a lot. I'm not the little girl I used to be."

I took in her face. Some things about her were still the same: freckled cheeks; round brown eyes; full, pouty lips. But her hair, which had once reached past her shoulders, was now short and wavy. And those pouty lips were lined in purple lipstick. Not a neon purple, but more like a dark, blue-black mix. Like the color of blackberries.

"I love your hair, but I can't believe you cut it." I wanted to touch her again, to make sure she was really standing in front of me. "It used to be so long."

"Thanks. Mom and Dad hate it." She began picking at her fingernails—her nail polish matched her lipstick. "It was their bright idea to send me down here for the summer. They must think Conway is too podunk for me to get into any real trouble."

"Conway isn't that small," I said. "I know it's nowhere near as big as Norfolk, but—"

"Please. Conway doesn't deserve to be mentioned in the same breath as Norfolk. I mean, you guys only have one bookstore. What kind of town only has one bookstore?"

"But Maddie—er, Madeline—we have plenty of bookstores."

"Christian ones don't count."

I laughed. One thing that definitely hadn't changed was her personality. She was still as stubborn as a lazy bulldog on a hot summer day.

She began to back away. "It was good catching up with you, Joshua, but I've got to get out of here. I need to get some studying in before I go to work."

"No . . . wait." I stepped toward her. "Can't you stick around for a while? I'd love to talk for a few minutes . . . to catch up."

I had so many questions. So much to talk about.

Like:

Why did you come to church dressed like that? Your parents would have a heart attack if they could see you.

Like:

Why are you back in Conway, if you hate it so much?

Like:

Why did you stop writing me? You promised, remember?

Madeline shook her head. "I don't know, Joshua. I should really get going—"

"I have a youth group meeting, but it'll only last a few minutes." My voice sounded airy and rushed. "Better yet, why don't you come to the meeting with me?"

"I don't think that's a good idea." Her eyes cut toward the building, then back at me. "I'm not really into organized religion."

She took a step backward. This time, I didn't follow.

"I mean, I believe in God and all. I just don't believe in the whole church thing anymore. Only reason I'm here now is because . . . well, let's just say that according to Dad, it's part of my penance." She placed her hands on her hips and jutted her chest out even farther. "I figured if he was going to force me to come to church, I was going to wear something that people would remember. What do you think?"

It took everything in my power not to let my gaze fall to her chest. "That's not funny, Madeline."

"Who said I was joking?" She nodded toward the church. "You should head to your meeting. You don't want to be late."

And then, just as suddenly as she had reappeared into my life, she vanished. I would have thought it was all a dream, except for the coffee-and-vanilla scent that lingered in the air.

* * *

"The sermon was okay, but I think I could have made it stronger. I just didn't get the reaction I wanted from the congregation. Maybe if I had focused a little more on Paul's plight."

Dad had been talking nonstop since we sat down for dinner, but I was too busy staring at the mound of roast beef on my plate to pay attention.

This was not the same Maddie Smith I knew five years ago. What had happened to the thirteen-year-old girl, all skin and bones? The girl I used to play hide-and-seek with behind the church? The girl with the blackberry-stained lips who promised we'd always be friends?

I'll tell you what had happened—she'd grown up.

"Joshua?" Dad leaned closer to me. "You awake? I was asking your opinion on the sermon."

I turned toward him. "I liked it," I said. "Everyone was

probably anxious to get home. Game four of the NBA Finals comes on this afternoon."

Dad ran his fingers through his hair. His temples had turned white long ago, and now the rest of his hair was following suit. "That's what's wrong with our people. Too busy watching MTV and ESPN to pray and learn the word."

"Isaiah, there's nothing wrong with enjoying music or sports." Mom dabbed at the corners of her mouth with a cloth napkin. "Or maybe you've forgotten about those golf clubs collecting dust in the garage."

Dad smiled. With all the clubs, clothes, and training videos he had collected over the years, you'd think he was an avid golf player. But he was so busy with church business, he only made it out to the golf course a few times a year, usually when some big-shot preacher was visiting. Of course, that didn't stop Dad from buying himself a new golf toy every year for his birthday. This year's present, a custom-made sand wedge, hadn't even made it out of its box.

"Lily, I like sports—and yes, golf is a real sport—as much as anyone else, but we're not in the business of creating the next Tiger Woods or Michael Jordan. We're in the business of saving souls." He glanced at me. "Unfortunately, too many of our members forget that."

Even though Dad hadn't said it, I knew he was thinking about the boys' basketball team that the church had sponsored this past spring. The team he grudgingly decided to support, at the request of a few of the more influential members of the congregation. The team that had lost every game of the season.

Dad sliced himself another piece of roast beef. "Sorry I wasn't able to sit in on the youth group meeting. How did it go?"

I peered at him out of the corner of my eye. "Some of the girls brought up the idea of a praise-dance ministry again."

Dad paused from eating but didn't look up from his plate. "You'd think with all the events you kids are planning for the Youth Revival, and with the upcoming retreat, you wouldn't need any other activities."

"But the Youth Revival only happens once a year, and we're just going to plain old Savannah for our retreat," I said. "The girls want something more—"

"Joshua, we've had this conversation before. The last thing I want is a bunch of hormonal sixteen-year-old girls gyrating in my sanctuary." He finally looked up from his plate. "The last thing *God* wants is a bunch of girls gyrating in *His* sanctuary."

I knew Dad was a preacher and all, but the way he talked sometimes, you'd think he knew God better than any other person on the planet. "Dad, gyrating isn't exactly what I'd call it. Plus, the girls think it'll be a good way to get other youth involved, especially since we weren't able to get enough girls to sign up for the basketball league."

"And what do you think?"

I think we should try it, I wanted to say. But I didn't

say it, because it wouldn't have done any good. Senior Pastor Wynn had already made up his mind.

I sighed. "I think we should focus on getting more youth to join the choir instead," I mumbled, feeling like Judas.

Mom fingered the string of shiny white pearls around her neck. "I couldn't help but notice you talking to some girl in the parking lot after church. She looked familiar, but I couldn't quite place her."

I was curious how Mom had seen us, when she was parked on the opposite side of where Madeline and I were talking. But being the good Christian boy that I was, I didn't mention this.

"I was talking to Madeline Smith."

Mom's eyes widened. "That was Maddie? She looks so . . . mature."

I frowned. "It's been five years since she's been back home. She's grown a little."

Mom stared off into space, a blank look on her face. "Little Maddie Smith," she said. "She used to be such a sweet girl—could quote the Bible better than most adults." Mom turned back to me. "I know y'all used to keep in touch. When's the last time you heard from her?"

I thought about all my unanswered letters. "It's been a while."

"Well, maybe that's for the best, because she certainly doesn't look like the girl I remember." Mom waved her fork in the air. "What was she thinking, wearing a dress like that to church? She should be ashamed of herself."

I tightened my grip on my knife. "Nowadays, girls wear stuff like that all the time."

"She's not just any girl," Mom said. "She's a preacher's daughter. There are some things she just can't do."

"But Mom—"

"Your mother's right, Joshua. I noticed her during my sermon, and I agree, what she wore was inappropriate." Dad's deep voice rang throughout the dining room. "Her father says she's been quite the problem child over the past few years."

I took a quick sip of water to wash away the dry, chalky taste in my throat. "Did you know she was back in town?"

He nodded. "Her father told me she'd be spending the summer with her aunt Gwendolyn. I made a few calls and was able to get her a job down at Yvonne Brockington's coffee shop."

That explained the coffee smell.

"I would have said something earlier, but first I wanted to see if she'd actually come to service," he said. "Greg warned me that she'd probably be more interested in making a scene than recommitting herself to her faith."

I pushed around a few grains of rice with my fork. "Do you know what happened to her? She's so . . . different now."

Dad swallowed the last of his roast beef. "Supposedly she got involved with some boy at that fancy boarding school her father sent her to, and things went downhill from there. She got accepted to Brown—even got a partial scholarship—but Greg refused to pay the rest of her tuition." Dad pushed his empty plate away from him. "According to Greg, he wasn't about to spend his hard-earned money on Maddie's schooling just to have her prancing around campus, wasting his money on tight skirts and black lipstick."

"Her dress wasn't that tight," I said. "And her lipstick is purple, not black."

"Purple, black, blue—it doesn't really matter," Mom said. "It breaks my heart every time I talk to Greg or Paulette—that girl seems to cause them more grief than any parent should have to bear." Mom shook her head. "We just have to keep praying for Maddie and hope she eventually gets all this nonsense out of her system."

Mom returned to eating her salad, but Dad just stared at me. "Maybe we should do more than just pray for her," he said.

"You want me to speak to her?" Mom asked. "I can probably find some time next—"

"Actually, I think Joshua should talk to her."

You would have thought I was born mute, as speechless as I was right then.

Mom placed her fork on her plate. "Isaiah, don't you think I'd be better suited to talk to her? I've been counseling young women for quite a few years."

"She and Joshua used to be best friends," Dad said. "If anyone could get through to her, he could. Maybe he could stop by the coffee shop one day and strike up a conversation."

Yeah, I could do that. I'd be happy to do that.

"And then what is he supposed to do? Tie her up and beat her over the head with a Bible?" Mom's voice was a controlled shout. "Joshua's only seventeen, Isaiah. He's not—"

"Joshua's a good kid, Lily. It'll take a lot more than a simple conversation to sway him off his path." Dad rose from the table. "I've got to run. I've got a meeting at the church in less than an hour, and I still have to finish preparing my notes. We can talk about this more tonight."

Mom watched Dad disappear down the hallway, the frown on her face deepening as each second passed. "I think I'm finished with dinner," she said after a few moments. "You want anything else to eat?"

I looked at the mountain of meat sitting on my plate. "Thanks, but I'm okay."

Mom rose from her chair but didn't move away from the table. "I know you want to impress your father, but you don't have to talk to Madeline if you don't want to. He's putting you in an uncomfortable situation."

"Really, I don't mind." I did my best to keep my voice cool and calm, to try to hide the fireworks popping off in my chest.

"Maybe I should rephrase that. *I* don't want you seeing Madeline." Mom squeezed the back of her chair, her fingers disappearing in its plush cream cushioning. "Madeline used to be one of the smartest, sweetest girls I knew, but that was a long time ago. There's no telling what type of person she is now."

I stared at Mom's hands, wondering if they would leave

a permanent imprint in the chair. "I just want to talk to her," I said. "We're Christians. It's our job to help people, right?"

She released her grip on the chair, then picked up her half-full plate. "That sounds like something your father would say." She headed toward the kitchen but paused at the doorway. "Fine, go talk to the girl if you want to. But remember—you can't save people who don't want to be saved."

A few seconds later, I heard glasses clinking in the sink and the rush of water from the faucet. I plopped my elbows onto the table and buried my head in my hands.

I probably should have been thinking about what I was going to say to Madeline—how I was going to lead her back to the path of the righteous—but all I could do was think about her lips. Their color. Their . . . taste.

I had no doubt that Madeline Smith needed saving. I just wasn't quite sure if I was interested in being her savior.

chapter 2

It had been four months since Jenn and I broke up—or rather, since she dumped me—but I still felt strange visiting the nursing home without her. Although it was *my* high school, not hers, that had adopted the Faith Nursing Home, she often came out and visited with me during the school year. Now that school was out, I was probably the only student who still came by during the summer months. Not that I minded—I really liked visiting the senior citizens. I just missed having someone to come visit them with me.

It wasn't just our trips to the nursing home that I missed. I missed playing Scrabble and watching old movies with her. I missed the way she laughed at my bad jokes. I missed seeing her at youth group meetings. I missed the way my parents would smile when she came over to visit.

Of course, I also missed all the making out, but I wasn't supposed to be focusing on the physical parts of the relationship, right? She wasn't a piece of meat. She was my girlfriend. My perfect girlfriend.

My perfect *ex*-girlfriend.

Even now, I could still hear her sweet, high-pitched voice as she gave me the news.

I'm sorry, Joshua, but I think we should break up. I want a boyfriend, not a saint.

Truthfully, I was a little surprised, but I assumed it'd be like any of our other arguments. She'd be mad for a few days, but she'd eventually get over it. I mean, yeah, compared to other guys, maybe I was a "good guy." But so what? She was a good girl. Good girls belonged with good guys.

But then three days without her calling turned into three weeks. Jenn even stopped coming to church, instead attending Catholic Mass with her father.

Charlotte, Tony's girlfriend, attended the same school as Jenn, so I constantly prodded her for information. All Charlotte would do was change the subject.

Finally, I broke down and called Jenn. And it was then that she told me she was seeing someone else.

Later, Tony and Charlotte told me that not only was Jenn dating her lab partner (who, incidentally, was a stud football player with hands big enough to rip a phone book in half), but she had *slept* with him.

Jennifer Anne Dowling—my perfect ex-girlfriend—had lost her virginity to someone else.

Of course, I was mad. No, not mad—livid. No, not livid—*incensed*. So what did I do?

I prayed for her soul.

And what's worse, I prayed for her new boyfriend's soul as well.

Why? Because the Bible said that premarital sex was wrong. Because I was supposed to forgive her for her transgressions. Because that was what my parents would have wanted me to do.

But even now, as I walked into the nursing home, all I wanted to do was find this new boyfriend of hers and smash my fist into his face. Then I wanted to find a new girlfriend and catch up on all the kissing and making out that I'd been missing out on.

Part of me even wanted to do more than make out.

But that wasn't going to happen, because I was Joshua Wynn, the preacher's son. I was supposed to be a shining example of what was good and righteous and wholesome in the world.

"Joshua, you okay?" Becca, the receptionist, asked as I signed in. "You look mad."

I took a deep breath and forced a smile. "I'm okay." I nodded toward the rec room. "Are they in there?"

"Of course. Where else would they be?"

I took a few more deep, calming breaths, then entered

the rec room. Leonard King and Mr. Rollins sat at a table in the corner, deep in a chess game. I hovered over Leonard's shoulder but didn't say anything. I had been visiting them long enough to know I should never interrupt them when they were playing chess.

Leonard scratched the stubble on his chin and leaned back. He muttered something under his breath and tapped his cane against the linoleum floor.

"Leonard, I'ma be dead by the time you make a move," Mr. Rollins grumbled from across the table. He took off his felt hat and fanned himself. "Just move your damn piece so we can get this game over with."

Leonard moved his leathery, wrinkled hand to the board and slid one of the black pieces to an adjoining square. "Your move," he said. "But just so you know, there ain't no way you can win."

I stared at the board. It was still full of black and white chess pieces.

Mr. Rollins popped the brake on his wheelchair and inched closer to the table. The wrinkles on his forehead intensified as he studied the board. After a few seconds, he scowled and threw his hat to the ground. "I'll be a sonofabitch. . . ."

As Mr. Rollins continued to curse to himself, I grabbed a chair from a nearby table and sat down. "I'm sorry I haven't been around more. Church stuff has been keeping me pretty busy."

Leonard waved off my apology. "You ain't missin' nothin' here," he said. "Rollins still hasn't won a game."

"I woulda won last week, if Beatrice hadn't knocked the board over," Mr. Rollins said. "You'd think she woulda found a way to lose some of that weight after all these years."

"I heard that, Carl Rollins," Ms. Beatrice yelled from across the room. For an eighty-something-year-old woman, she had very good hearing.

"What's a youngun like you doing here on a nice summer day like this?" Leonard asked. "You should be out courtin'."

I picked up one of the chess pieces—the bishop. "I don't have much time for dating."

"What happened to that girl you used to bring over here?" Leonard asked.

"Jenn?" I shook my head. "We broke up. But I thought I told you that before."

"Leonard can't remember to wipe his own ass, much less what you told him a few months ago," Mr. Rollins said.

Leonard chuckled. "Well, I still remember how to whup your butt playing chess." He turned to me. "Sorry to hear about the girl. She seemed nice."

Mr. Rollins elbowed me. "Don't worry 'bout it. I've had four wives, and none of 'em were worth the trouble it took to keep 'em happy. You're better off being by yourself." Mr. Rollins opened his mouth like he was going to continue, but instead erupted into a series of harsh, wheezing coughs.

Everyone in the room held their breath. Mr. Rollins

had lung cancer, and ever since he had stopped his chemo treatments, his coughing fits had dramatically intensified to the point where it was almost painful to watch.

Mr. Rollins finally stopped struggling long enough to suck in a few breaths. "What the hell are y'all staring at?" he mumbled. "Why don't one of y'all get me a cup of water or somethin'?"

Just then, one of the nurses walked in holding a paper cup. Mr. Rollins extended his trembling hand, took the cup, and then swallowed a gulp of water.

"You'd better lie down for a while, Rollins," Leonard said. "You're liable to cough up your last good lung if you don't take it easy."

Mr. Rollins shook his head. "Admit it—you're just scared to play another game."

The nurse placed her hand on Mr. Rollins's shoulder. "I should take you to your room. You need your medicine."

Mr. Rollins narrowed his eyes at the nurse before looking at me. "See what I mean? These women won't do anything but ruin your life. Always trying to tell you what to do and where to go."

The nurse began to wheel Mr. Rollins away. "Do you need anything?" I asked him.

"Naw, I'm good, but thanks for offering." Then he winked. "But I wouldn't be opposed to the nurse here givin' me one of them sponge baths."

The nurse swatted him on the arm. "You should be ashamed of yourself," she said, although she was laughing. "You're too old to be so bad."

He grunted. "What the hell's the point of living if you can't be bad?"

* * *

My trip to the nursing home was the only part of my day that went according to plan. Choir practice ran almost an hour longer than I had anticipated, forcing me to cancel my committee meeting, which meant *I'd* be the one up late tonight working on the agenda for the Youth Revival. I was supposed to shoot hoops with Tony tomorrow, but I needed to stop by Foot Locker to buy a new pair of wristbands. And though I had a truckload of books to read for my advanced English class, I hadn't come close to setting foot inside the library.

So if I had so many things to do, why did I suddenly have a hankering for a cup of coffee?

I ignored the time on my cell phone as I switched off the ringer and walked into Yvonne's Coffee Shop. An older woman stood behind a counter filled with cakes and cookies. "What can I get for you?" she asked.

"I'm actually looking for Madeline," I said. "Is she working tonight?"

The woman squinted at me for a second before turning toward the rear of the shop. "Madeline, come on out. The Wynn boy is here to see you."

The Wynn boy? I looked down at my chest to see if somehow I had been walking around with my name attached to the front of my shirt.

"Hey, Joshua," Madeline said as she exited the back of the store. Just like a few days ago, her lips and fingernails were painted dark purple. She had traded in her dress for jeans and a tank top, although one could argue that the tank top was more revealing than the dress. "What are you doing here?"

"I figured I'd drop by for a cup of coffee on my way home."

"Then what can I get you?"

Good question. I looked over the menu. I hated coffee. I couldn't understand why someone would want to drink something so bitter.

All that being said, I was a guy—a man. *A manly man.* I couldn't order one of those fluffy iced latte-type drinks. Not in front of Madeline.

"Let me have a regular coffee." I pulled a few dollars from my pocket and handed them to her.

"No charge." The older woman walked up to the counter and pushed my money back toward me. "After everything Pastor Wynn's done for me, the least I can do is give you a free cup of coffee."

"Thanks," I mumbled. I tried to come up with a name to match her face, but my mind was blank. She wasn't Yvonne, that much I knew.

"I bet you're gonna be just like your daddy," she continued. "Only a matter of time before you're up in that pulpit, preaching the word."

I shook my head. "I don't know if preaching's what I'm supposed to do—"

"Nonsense," she said. "You're made to be a preacher. It's in your blood."

"Carla, maybe you're getting a little ahead of yourself. Joshua hasn't even finished high school." Madeline winked at me as she grabbed one of the extra-large paper cups. "Why don't you find a seat? I'll bring your drink to you."

I nodded and escaped from the counter. As I headed to a table in the corner of the café, I made a mental note of Carla's face. Mount Calvary had grown in recent years, almost to the point where Dad was thinking about starting another Sunday morning service. Growth was a good thing—not knowing all the parishioners just happened to be a bad side effect.

A few minutes after I sat down, Madeline approached the table with a black book bag hanging from her shoulder and a small tray firmly in her grasp. Her top had worked its way up slightly, so her pierced belly button was exposed. And I was sure her jeans would fall from her hips at any second, on account of how low they sat on her waist.

"I was about to take my break when you walked in," she said. "Mind if I join you?"

"Of course not." I rose from the table and pulled out a chair for her. "Now, who exactly is Carla?"

"Yvonne's sister," she said. "She's been attending your church for almost six months. Don't you recognize her?"

I slumped back into my seat. "We have so many members now, it's hard to keep track of everyone."

Madeline placed two cups, a few packets of sugar and cream, and a slice of carrot cake on the table, then melted into the chair across from me. "It gets old, doesn't it? All the opinions on the type of person you're supposed to be, the type of life you're supposed to live?"

I nodded and wondered if she was talking about me or her.

She pushed the carrot cake to the center of the table. "I didn't know if you liked cream or sugar, so I brought both. And feel free to have some of my cake, as long as you don't mind eating fat-free. I could stand to lose some weight."

I looked into my steaming cup of muck-colored coffee. "I think you're perfect just like you are."

"I wish you'd been around to tell that to my old gym teacher. Or better yet, some of my past boyfriends." Madeline paused as she bowed her head and whispered a few words. As she prayed, I noticed a small silver cross hanging around her neck.

I didn't even realize she had finished praying until she cleared her throat. "Hey, I know they're nice to look at, but I do have a face."

My body temperature skyrocketed as I quickly averted my gaze from her chest. "I'm sorry, I know how that looked. I happened to notice the cross around your neck as you were praying—wait a minute, why were you praying? I didn't think you believed in God."

She rolled her eyes. "Joshua, were you even listening to me last Sunday? I'm not very religious, but I'm extremely spiritual," she said. "I'm still a Christian. I just don't go to church."

"Why not?"

"Most of the people who go to church are hypocrites. Plus, like Emily Dickinson said, why have the Sabbath at church when I can have it at home?"

"Well, I don't know about Emily Dickinson, but according to God, it's our duty to fellowship with other Christians."

"Hebrews, chapter ten, verse twenty-five." Madeline broke off a piece of carrot cake and popped it into her mouth. "You should drink your coffee. It's getting cold."

I took a timid sip and almost died from the bitterness. "This is the best coffee I've had in years."

Technically, that wasn't a lie, being that I hadn't had any in almost two years.

"So who was your friend in the choir stand?" she asked. "The one who kept whispering to you and looking in my direction."

I dumped four packets of sugar into my cup. "Noticed that, huh?"

"Kind of hard not to notice when almost every male in the choir stand is staring at you." She swiped some icing onto her finger. "But I probably asked for it. I shouldn't have worn something so . . ."

"Tight-fitting?"

"I was going to say *slutty,* but your word sounds a lot better." She smiled, and one hundred goose bumps exploded on my arm. "You were the only guy up there not staring at me. I don't know whether I should be upset or flattered."

"Thanks, I think." I took another sip of my coffee. "The

guy sitting next to me was my friend Tony. He moved here a few years after you left." I nodded toward her book bag, eager to change the subject. "What classes are you taking this summer?"

"English literature and Latin."

"English lit," I said. "Maybe I should have you write some of my essays for me. I should be at the library now."

Madeline smirked. "Don't tell me you're playing hooky. What would your mom say if she knew you were hanging out with me?"

"You don't even want to know."

I had meant for my words to come off light and funny, but I could hear the dark undertones to my voice. I was afraid Madeline could hear the same thing.

She reached into her book bag. "Maybe I can save you a trip." She pulled out a book and handed it to me.

"*Maus*?" I flipped open the book. "You've got to be kidding."

"What's wrong?"

I pointed to the page I was on. "This is a comic book."

"That comic book won a Pulitzer Prize. And it's called a graphic novel, not a comic book."

"Looks like a comic book to me."

She shook her head and threw her hands up. "Art Spiegelman did something that had never been done before—he used a supposedly 'simple' art form to successfully convey the horrors of the Holocaust." She grabbed my hand and squeezed hard. "It's groundbreaking. It's revolutionary. And to be honest, it's a fucking awesome piece of literature." Madeline took a quick breath. "This is only the first book. You really need to pick up the second one as well."

Madeline continued to rant about the wonders of the book, but I had long ago stopped listening. My mind was stuck on one word—one very distinct word—that I wasn't expecting to hear.

Finally, she stopped and looked at me, her eyebrows bunched tight on her forehead. "What's wrong?" She brought her hands to her face. "Do I have icing on my mouth or something?"

"Since when did you start cursing?"

"What?"

"You cursed. You said the f word."

She laughed. "Don't tell me you've never heard the word *fuck* before."

I gritted my teeth. "I've heard it plenty of times. I just never heard it from you."

She shrugged. "Sorry."

"You used to say that people only cursed because they couldn't find any other way to express themselves."

"I used to say a lot of things," she said. "Things change. People change."

"Apparently so."

We were silent for a few seconds as Madeline drank her tea and I struggled with another sip of coffee. I had known Madeline for years, but now a complete stranger sat across from me.

Madeline finished her drink and leaned closer to me.

"Why are you really here? And don't say it's for the coffee. I've seen people more eager to drink bleach." I could smell the sweetness of the carrot cake on her breath. "You trying to save me?"

"I'm not—"

"Don't lie," she said. "Your dad sent you down here, didn't he?"

I shook my head. "It's not like that. I'm worried about you, that's all. I heard things weren't going so easy for you."

She crossed her arms. "What exactly have you heard about me?"

"My dad said you had some boy troubles. And that you weren't going to Brown anymore."

"And . . . ?"

"That's it. Is there more?"

Madeline's grimace melted into a melancholy smile. "It's not anything you'd want to hear about."

I studied her face, hoping for something that would clue me in to the mystery her life had become. "Just tell me what's wrong. What made you stop going to church? Why aren't you going to Brown?"

Madeline began stacking the cups on her tray. "Joshua, thanks for coming by, but I don't think we should hang out," she said. "I'm not some damsel in distress that needs saving. I like me just the way I am." She rose from the table. "Plus, I have the feeling that I'm probably not a good influence on you. Our worlds don't really mesh anymore."

"But—"

"No buts, no exceptions." She picked up her tray. "Read the book. I promise you'll like it."

"When do you want me to return it?"

"Keep it. I've already read it four times." She started toward the counter. "Good night, Joshua," she called over her shoulder.

I stared at Madeline for a few more minutes as she cleaned up the counter and did an outstanding job of avoiding eye contact with me. After a few moments, I finally left.

I didn't bother looking at my watch as I walked to my car, her book in my hand. I knew it was late, and I was sure Mom was freaking out.

I started the car and glanced at my phone. Three messages, all from home.

Yep, Mom was worried, all right. But that made me wonder: Did Madeline have someone who worried about her as much as my mother worried about me?

chapter 3

"So you left?"

I took the basketball from Tony and dribbled it a few times. Even though our pitiful season was over, Tony and I still liked to shoot hoops whenever we had the time. "What else was I supposed to do? Madeline made it pretty clear she wasn't interested in carrying on the conversation."

Tony planted himself in front of me and stuck his hand in my face. I blew past him and streaked toward the goal. As I leapt into the air, the basketball elevated out of my fingers and floated through the rim.

It should be a sin to score a basket so easily.

Tony grabbed the ball. "Show-off."

As soon as Tony's father had found out the church was starting a basketball team, he ran out and purchased one of those high-priced, NBA-endorsed goals. Tony practiced every day for two months, and sure enough, he made the team.

Of course, everyone who tried out made the team. We were supposed to have twelve players on the roster, but only ten guys showed up for tryouts.

Rachel, Tony's younger sister, had practiced even more than him, and unlike her brother, she became a pretty good basketball player. She would have definitely made the team if we had had enough girls to form one.

Tony attempted to dribble the ball a few times. "So when are you going back to Yvonne's?" he asked. "I sure wouldn't mind tagging along."

I posted myself in front of Tony. "Don't you have a girl-friend?"

"Hey, there ain't no law against window-shopping." Tony shot the ball over me and hit nothing but air. "If it was me, I'd be at that coffee shop every day. With a body like that, that girl's made to be admired."

"She's got a name, you know." I retrieved the ball before it rolled into the street. "And don't talk about her like that. Madeline can't help the way she's built. It doesn't make her a slut or anything." I threw the ball at him, a little harder than I anticipated. He barely had enough time to get his hands up to catch it.

Tony palmed the basketball and looked as if he was thinking about hurling it back at me. "Why are you getting so defensive? I never said anything about her being a slut." He softly lobbed the ball to me. "But you got to admit—she's supersexy."

I rolled my eyes. "Do you ever talk about anything other than sex?"

He smiled. "What else am I supposed to talk about?"

I dribbled the ball between my legs. "Well, since we're already talking about sex ... are you and Charlotte still ..."

Tony laughed as I struggled with words I couldn't bring myself to say. "You're such a prude," he said. "But don't worry—me and Charlotte aren't going all the way."

"Technically, it's still considered sex."

"Thanks for the public service announcement, but I ain't in the mood for a lecture." He tried to steal the ball from me, but half-dead snails moved faster than he did.

I dribbled to a spot about fifteen feet from the rim and took another shot. The basketball banked off the backboard and sank through the net.

"Josh, you should really try out for the school basketball team." Tony collapsed in the grass at the edge of the driveway. I dropped down next to him. "I mean, you're good enough to be a starter. You'd be the most popular guy at school."

"Do you know how much the varsity team practices? I don't have that much time to commit to sports." I grabbed my water bottle and took a swig. "I shouldn't even be here."

"What is it you have to do now? Let me guess—the ladies at the nursing home are in need of an extra bridge player. Or better yet, somebody's cat is stuck in a tree."

I grunted in reply.

"It's not your job to save everyone, you know," he said. "If you really want to help someone, start with yourself. When's the last time you went out?"

"Not sure. I don't really keep up with it."

"Well, I'm sure you're already aware of this, but Jenn will probably be at Charlotte's birthday party next week. She plans to bring her boyfriend."

Of course, I wasn't surprised. Charlotte invited everyone to her parties. I just wasn't sure if it was because she liked the attention or the gifts.

"I don't know what Jenn sees in him," Tony continued. "He's a loser. And he's . . . big."

I perked up. "You mean he's fat?"

"Actually, I meant big as in muscular," Tony said. "But give him a few more years, and I'm sure all that muscle will turn into flab."

Leave it to Tony to make me feel worse than I had before. "Why should I care? It's not like I'm going to the party."

"There'll be a lot of good-looking prep-school girls there."

"I had one, remember. It didn't work out." I glanced at my watch. "Don't you have a date tonight?"

"Guess that means you don't want to talk about it anymore." Tony stood and then helped me to my feet. "Hey, why don't you come along? We're just going to the movies."

I faked a shocked look. "How are you supposed to get your groove on with me hanging around?"

"For you, I'll make the sacrifice," he said. "It'll be fun."

"Haven't you heard that three makes a crowd?"

"I could probably get Charlotte to invite one of her friends."

"Four makes an even bigger crowd."

He shook his head. "I don't get you, Josh. You say you want to be normal, but you don't do the stuff normal kids do."

I followed Tony into the kitchen. "So what—I have to curse, drink, and have sex to be considered normal?"

Tony's arm jerked sharply as he opened his refrigerator. "Now see, it's when you say things like that that people don't want to be around you. I know you mean well, but you can come off as pretty damn self-righteous sometimes."

I frowned. I probably sounded as bad as some of the holy rollers at church. "Sorry, I don't mean to come off as judgmental. It's just pretty clear in the Bible that—"

"Josh, I know you love the Lord and everything, but come on. You can pray and ask for forgiveness when you're old. Now's when you're supposed to be enjoying life." Tony grabbed a two-liter bottle of Coke from the shelf, and quicker than you could say *unhygienic*, he tilted his head back and started guzzling down the soda.

As I tried to formulate a rebuttal, I heard footsteps behind me. "You know, we do have glasses."

I turned around. "Rachel?"

The girl who had just walked into the room *sounded* like Rachel, but she sure didn't look like her. The Rachel I knew always wore scuffed-up Nikes and jeans, not frilly summer dresses. And . . . was she wearing makeup?

Rachel smiled. "Hey, Joshua. I'm sorry Tony is acting so uncivilized."

Tony paused long enough from his guzzlefest to let out a large belch. Then he winked at me and brought the bottle back to his lips.

"You're disgusting," Rachel said. "I can't believe you did that in front of a guest!"

Tony finished off the soda and tossed the empty plastic bottle toward the trash can. It fell five feet short.

"What are you talking about? Josh ain't a guest." He looked his sister up and down. "Is that lipstick?" he asked. "Since when did Mom start letting you wear makeup?"

"I'm fifteen years old. I'm not a little girl anymore." Rachel brushed her hair from her face. "And it's cherry lip gloss, not lipstick."

Tony picked up the soda bottle and deposited it in the trash. "You know, if you're so grown-up now, why do you still sleep in Winnie the Pooh pajamas—"

"Antonio Myers! I can't believe you just said that!" Rachel balled up her fists and marched toward her brother, her lips curled into a snarl.

Tony sprinted around the table so that six chairs and a huge hunk of mahogany separated him from his sister. "Josh, I think that's my cue to leave. I'd show you out, but I've got an emotional fifteen-year-old who wants to rip my limbs from their sockets." With that, he turned and dashed down the hallway.

"You'd better run!" Rachel yelled after him, her fingers clenched into brother-beating fists. She looked down at her feet. "I could have caught him, if not for these stupid sandals."

I laughed. Tony was a snail on the basketball court, but given the proper motivation, he was as quick and nimble as a slightly overweight cheetah.

"Don't mind Tony," I said. "Some people have a hard time growing up." I took a closer look at her face. "What's with the makeup?"

"Charlotte thought it was time I started looking less like a tomboy and more like a girl." She tucked her hair behind her ears and tilted her face to me. "What do you think?"

"It looks good. It brings out the brown in your eyes." To be honest, the bright red lip gloss looked a little thick and uneven on her lips, but given her reaction to Tony's comments, I wasn't about to say that.

Rachel's grin widened. "You really like it?" She giggled and brought her hands to her face. "Charlotte took me to the mall yesterday and helped me pick it out."

As much as I didn't like talking about makeup, I figured the more she talked about it, the less likely she would be to bring up the idea of forming a praise-dance team.

"You and Charlotte are getting pretty close, aren't you?"

Rachel nodded. "She invited me to her birthday party, but I don't think Mom'll let me go. Are you going?"

"Yeah, unfortunately."

Rachel's shoulders slumped and her lips turned into a mini-frown.

"Why are you so dressed up?" I asked.

"I've got a date tonight."

It seemed like everyone had more of a social life than I did. Tony was having *almost-sex*, Rachel was dating, and Madeline was—Lord, there was no telling *what* Madeline was doing.

"Well, it's not a real date," she continued. "A bunch of us are going to the movies. I don't like any of the boys who are going, though."

"Good, because you're too young to be interested in boys anyway." Finally, someone was acting like they had some common sense. "You can't trust them."

She giggled again. She had been doing that a lot lately. "Don't be silly. Of course I like boys. I'm just not interested in any of the boys we're going out with tonight. They're less mature than Tony."

"*All* guys are immature." I inched away from Rachel. It smelled like she had doused herself in strawberry perfume. "All they want is sex."

"I know. Every time I turn around, some pimple-faced perv is trying to cram his tongue down my throat."

"You're kissing boys now?"

"Weren't you kissing girls by the time you were fifteen?"

I wasn't, but that wasn't anything I wished to share.

"You know, kissing isn't the worst thing in the world." She readjusted the plastic bracelets on her skinny wrist. "What Tony and Charlotte do is a lot worse."

I froze. "What does that mean?"

"It means Charlotte can't keep a secret to save her life. I know she and Tony have been . . ." She shuddered. "She must really like him. There's no way I'd do *you-know-what* to a boy."

I gulped. "Listen, maybe you're mistaken. I'm sure they're not doing anything—"

"Joshua, quit treating me like a kid!" She crossed her arms. "She gives him blow jobs in the backseat of her car. That clear enough?"

I felt my cheeks starting to burn. For the second time in a week, I'd heard someone say something that I never expected to hear come from their mouth.

"Um . . . I'd better get out of here." I almost tripped over my feet as I headed for the door. "I hope you have fun on your date tonight."

Rachel followed me. "Sorry, Joshua. I didn't mean to embarrass you."

I paused at the door. "I'm just a little shocked. I didn't know you knew about things like that."

"Just because I'm not doing it doesn't mean I don't know about it," she said. "Don't you watch TV?"

* * *

Mom and Dad weren't home when I got there; they were, of course, at church. There was always another meeting, another choir practice, another Bible study to attend, and as the first family of Mount Calvary, we were always expected to be there. Tonight, the senior ushers' board was hosting a banquet, and my father was the keynote speaker.

I took a shower, fully intending to throw on a suit and head to the church. But for some reason, I couldn't bring myself to put on one of those god-awful, heavy-starched, long-sleeved white shirts. Instead, I called the pizza place. Once the pizza arrived, I poured myself a large glass of Coke, planted myself in front of the TV, and flipped to some music videos.

I might have been a rising senior, but to most people, I probably seemed like the most naive person in the world. Everyone else was getting *some* sort of sexual experience, while it looked like I happily stood on the sidelines.

Well, just to set the record straight, I wasn't happy.

It had taken a while—almost seven months—but I eventually built up the courage to where I could make out with Jenn without feeling like a hypocrite or a fool. I created rules for myself: I could slide my hand under her shirt, but not under her bra. I could squeeze the nipple, but only three times before I had to move my hand. Anywhere below the navel was strictly off-limits.

Unlike Tony, I saw a huge difference between making out (which I enjoyed very much) and sleeping with someone. The church was clear: Premarital sex was wrong. On the other hand, I liked to believe that making out was merely . . . *discouraged.* Yes, lust was a sin, but I hoped that God might opt to be a little lenient with me on this commandment, especially given my otherwise upright behavior.

Plus, Dad had taught me a long time ago that church leaders couldn't practice what they didn't preach. Which was why Dad didn't curse, drink, or smoke. And likewise, why I didn't curse, drink, or smoke, and why I made out but didn't have sex.

But just because I wasn't doing it didn't mean I didn't think about it. A lot.

After I finished my food, I flipped off the television and headed to my room. I didn't have time to feel sorry for myself. I had an enormous amount of work to do, including writing the essay I had been avoiding all week.

I picked up the comic—no, graphic novel—that Madeline had given me. Why was I even contemplating reading it? Something told me that Mrs. Stover wouldn't exactly be thrilled to find out I had written an essay on a comic book.

Against my better judgment, I read the first page. Twenty-two pages later, I was interrupted by a rap on my door.

I quickly closed the book, as if it was an issue of *Playboy,* and stuffed it under my pillow. "Come in."

Mom entered the room. I was surprised she could move her lips, her mouth was so tight across her face. "What are you doing home? Since you never showed up at the church, I figured you had gone out with Tony."

I sat up. "Tony's hanging out with his girlfriend," I said. "I decided it would be best to stay in. I have a lot of reading to do."

"So I see." Mom's gaze floated to the edge of my bed, where a corner of the graphic novel jutted from underneath my pillow. She walked over to the bed and grabbed the book. "Since when did you start reading comic books?"

"It's called a graphic novel."

She flipped through a few pages of the book before handing it back to me. "And this is for school?"

"A friend lent it to me. It's part of my summer reading assignment."

Mom sat beside me, her skin smelling like baby powder and White Diamonds perfume. "I'm glad you're committed to your studies, but I have to admit, I was hoping you wouldn't be here when we got home. You should be hanging out with your friends."

"Like I said, Tony was going to the movies with his girlfriend."

"What about the other kids in the youth group? Maybe y'all could have done something."

That was the tragic flaw in Mom's thinking. There was a big difference between being *friendly* with someone and being their *friend*. Just because I knew a lot of people didn't automatically mean we were best buddies.

"Maybe another time," I said. "I'm really behind on my assignment."

Mom rose from the bed. She teetered in the middle of the room for a few seconds, her gaze glued on a piece of fuzz at the base of my desk.

"Mom? Is everything okay?"

She cleared her throat. "I figured it might be a good idea for us to chat for a spell, but to be honest, it's a lot harder talking to you now that you've grown up so much." She cut her eyes toward the door. "Your father should be the one discussing this with you, but he's too busy saving the world." She pulled her lips into a pained smile. "It's just that—it's been four months since you broke up with Jennifer. I'm surprised you haven't talked to me or your father about it."

This conversation had been building for quite a while. I think Mom and Dad liked Jenn even more than I did.

"It wasn't working out," I said. "We had different interests." *Different interests*—that was a mild way of putting it.

She twisted her wedding band around her finger. "I know it's tough being a teenager. Sometimes, your body gets the urge to do things you know are wrong."

I groaned. I was afraid Mom was going to slip into another talk about the birds and the bees. Like with this conversation, *she* had been the one to finally break it down to me, on account of Dad always being conveniently unavailable.

"You and Jennifer were getting really close," she continued, oblivious to the scowl on my face. "And it's understandable that, being a young man, you may have wanted to do some things she wasn't ready to do."

Someone, please shoot me now.

"I know how it feels to be your age. Lord knows, I wasn't always a preacher's wife. In my younger days, I used to—"

"Mom, please." I picked up the graphic novel. "I really want to finish this book tonight."

"Oh—of course. I'll let you get back to your reading." She looked almost as eager to end the conversation as I was. "I just wanted you to know I'm available if you ever want to talk."

"Thanks. I'll keep that in mind."

I was sure she meant well, but there was no way I was going to talk to Mom about Jenn. How would it sound, me telling her I got dumped because I was too stupid to sleep with my girlfriend? Preacher's son or not, it still sounded lame.

Mom walked to the door, then paused. "I meant to ask—how did it go with Madeline? I heard you stopped by Yvonne's yesterday."

I frowned. *How did she . . .*

"Carla told your father, and he told me," she said. "I heard it didn't go so well."

I glanced at Madeline's book. "I can't believe how much she's changed."

"It's hard, isn't it, seeing old friends barrel down a path you can't follow," Mom said. "But Madeline's a smart girl. I'm confident that with enough time, and enough prayer, she'll eventually find her way back to us."

"Well, I haven't quite given up on her yet. I'm going to try again—"

"It's not a matter of giving up on her, Joshua. It's recognizing that she's not ready to accept our help."

"But are you sure—"

"I'm positive." Mom's voice could punch holes through steel. "You've done all you can do. Now you have to put the rest in God's hands."

I bit my lip and looked away. How could she be so sure

there was no point in trying again? She felt I had done all I could do, but did God feel the same way? *I* surely didn't.

"Joshua?"

I looked back at Mom. "Maybe you're right," I said. "I suppose we'll just have to pray for her."

She stared at me. "So you're not going to see her anymore, right?"

I nodded. "I won't see her anymore."

And just like that, I lied to my mother for the first time.

A few wrinkles shot into Mom's forehead. Maybe she could hear the untruthfulness in my voice. "You're not . . . interested in her, are you?"

I shook my head a lot harder than necessary. "Of course not." Lie number two. "I'm just worried about her."

The frown disappeared from her face. "Let me know if you want to talk—about Jennifer or Madeline or anything else."

Mom left, and I returned to the graphic novel.

It was quite simple, lying to my mother. In fact, it was so easy, I wondered why I had waited until now to do it.

chapter 4

One day later, I stood outside Yvonne's Coffee Shop. Although it was almost ten o'clock at night, the high humidity and nonexistent breeze made it feel like noon.

I tucked Madeline's book underneath my arm, wiped my hands on my jeans, and entered the coffee shop, which was almost empty. Madeline sat in the corner, scribbling away on a notepad.

She narrowed her eyes as I approached. "Joshua, what are you doing here? Shouldn't you be out trying to convert the masses?"

I held up the book. "I came to return this."

"I gave it to you. I already read it, remember."

I somehow found the courage to step closer to the table. "I just wanted you to know, I really liked the book. It made me think."

That made her eyes soften. A little. "Really? Or are you saying that because you know it's what I want to hear?"

Butterflies fluttered in my stomach. "*Maus* is an amazing book. It was so . . . *real*. I never knew a graphic novel could be so powerful."

"And you said it was just a comic book." She finally smiled. "It just proves you can't judge a book by its cover."

I took her smile as an invitation to sit down. "I spent all afternoon reading." I pulled some folded sheets from inside the book. "I even wrote an essay on it."

"You wrote me an essay?" She snatched the papers out of my hand and crammed them to her face. "Is this how preachers' kids pick up girls nowadays?"

"I'm not trying to pick you up," I said, trying to ignore the great view I had of her chest. "And the essay isn't for you, it's for my class. I just figured you'd enjoy reading it."

"Do I look like I get my kicks from reading book reports?" Then she cocked her head and laughed, loud enough that the handful of people in the shop glanced our way. "Actually, I *do* like reading essays. I guess I'm a closet bibliophile."

I sat there, unsure how to respond.

"A bibliophile is a book lover," she said.

"I would have figured that out eventually."

"I bet you thought it had something to do with being

into porn, didn't you. Of course, that doesn't mean a bibliophile *isn't* into porn."

Good Lord, did she just say that?

Then the smile vanished from her face. "Seriously, did you write this paper thinking I'd forget our last conversation? Because if you think—"

"I promise, I just want to talk about the book." I held up my empty hands to try to show how defenseless I really was. "Well, maybe we can talk about some other stuff as well, but I won't bring up anything about you going back to church."

Her frown stayed in place. "I don't know, Joshua."

I focused on her mouth. She wore the same purple lipstick as before, which gave me an idea. "How about this?" I spit on my palms, rubbed them together, and then crossed my heart. "I promise, we won't talk about anything you don't want to discuss."

Madeline's eyes flashed open. "You remember that?"

"Of course. Don't you?"

"Well, I . . ." She ran her fingers through her hair. "That was such a long time ago. How old were we?"

"I was five when you taught me. And I didn't want to do it at first, because—"

"—because you thought you could get cooties from it!" She slapped the table. "I can't believe you remember that!"

For a second, Madeline looked like she did five years ago—full of smiles and laughter. "Do you . . ." I cleared my throat. "Do you remember the last time we made that pledge?"

Madeline dropped her gaze. "By the blackberry bush." She traced her finger along the rim of her cup. "Of course I remember."

"We promised we'd write each other." If I was braver, I would have grabbed her and forced her to look at me. "And we did, for a while. Then one day I wrote you, and you never wrote back."

"I know—"

"So then I wrote you again. And then again after that." I shook my head. "Finally I got the hint."

She looked up. "Joshua, I didn't mean for you to take it like that. I wanted to write you, I really did." She fingered the cross hanging from her neck. "Things got so busy. So complicated . . ."

I could almost see her words dissolving into the air. "Well, here's your chance to make it up to me. Read my essay and tell me what you think."

Her eyes twinkled. "How can a girl refuse an offer like that?" She turned to the paper but quickly looked back up. "You want a cup of coffee or something? Maybe tea?"

I gagged at the thought of another bitter cup of coffee. "I'd better pass."

"Try this." She pushed her cup across the table. "I think you'll like it."

I picked up the cup—whose lip had been marked with numerous purple smudges—and peered at the seemingly endless well of coffee. It looked a lot lighter than the stuff I had drunk before. Finding a lipstick-free spot on the rim,

I took a sip and was surprised by how smooth it tasted. "Hey, this isn't so—"

"Shhh. I'm reading here."

I continued drinking Madeline's coffee while I watched her read. Her lips moved ever so slightly as her gaze floated over the paper. I stole a glance at her notebook. I couldn't tell what she was writing—maybe it was poetry, maybe it was song lyrics. Whatever it was, she was composing it with purple ink.

She looked up from the paper. "You could do better."

I was a little hurt. "You think? I spent three hours working on that paper."

"Then it sounds like you wasted a lot of time." She handed the report back to me and took her cup. "If I wanted a play-by-play account of what happened in the novel, I'd read CliffsNotes. What I want to know is what you thought about the novel. How'd it make you feel? What was it telling you?" She pointed at my paper. "All that report is doing is regurgitating someone else's thoughts."

I stared at the paper. Three hours down the drain.

"Don't feel so bad." She rose from the table. "Let me grab some more coffee. Then we'll really figure out what's rattling around in that head of yours."

* * *

One hour and two cups of coffee later, I felt like Madeline and I had dissected every page of that book.

During the entire conversation, Madeline's voice jumped around like a boxer. One second, she'd be jabbing at me with questions. Other times, she'd lay one of her own views on me like she was going for a knockout.

When I read the book, I had only seen the words and pictures on the page. But with Madeline, everything took on an entirely different meaning.

It was amazing. *She* was amazing.

"This was fun," she said after finishing the last of her coffee. "You need to read the second book of the series. Then we can really talk."

I looked into my cup and was sad to see that I had finished as well. I pushed it to the side. "So I gather this means you're glad you didn't kick me out?"

She grinned. "Maybe I was a little harsh the other day. It's just that I've been burned by so many people. . . ." She shook her head. "Ah, never mind. What's done is done." Then she grabbed my hand and gave it a squeeze. "I'm really glad you came by. I forgot how easy it is to talk to you."

And maybe it was because of the way her skin felt against mine, or the way her smile seemed to radiate joy, or maybe it was the vanilla scent that lulled me into a false sense of security, but I was suddenly hit with a brilliant—and utterly stupid—idea.

"Hey, if you're not doing anything next Friday, maybe we could go to a party together."

Madeline slid her hand away from mine and twisted her mouth into a half smile, half frown. "Joshua Wynn, did you just ask me out?"

"No, of course not," I babbled. "It's just that Tony's girlfriend is having a big party for her seventeenth birthday. . . ."

"Thanks, but I think I'll pass. As much as I like hanging out with you, I figured we'd just get coffee every once in a while. Maybe watch a good movie or something."

I quickly nodded. "Yeah, I'll probably skip the party as well."

"Joshua, you will do no such thing."

"But—"

"Let me guess—you always feel out of place at house parties. Everyone's drinking and laughing, while you stand in the corner, trying to blend in with the furniture."

She was dead right, and I hated her for it. "Thanks for making me sound even more pathetic."

She patted my hand, and I had to admit, her touch made me feel a little better. "Think how I felt when I moved to Norfolk. I was a church girl, plus I didn't know anybody. It was almost six months before I was invited to my first real party." Madeline rose from the table, her hips exposed again thanks to another pair of gravity-defying jeans. "Sometimes you have to force people to see you differently. If not, you'll always be the good preacher's kid."

I followed her to the counter. "And how'd you pull off getting people to see you differently?"

Madeline kept her back to me. "I'm not really a good example of what to do." She glanced at her watch. "Wow, I didn't realize how late it was. I need to clean up before my ride gets here." She walked over to the wall and flicked the light switch. Automatically, the few people left in the café began packing away their books and shutting down their laptops.

"Creepy how they do that, isn't it? Kind of like Pavlov's dogs." She finally looked at me. "Thanks for stopping by. . . ."

"Since I'm already here, why don't you let me drop you off at home?" I didn't want the night to end. I *refused* to let the night end. "Really, I don't mind. It'll save your aunt a trip."

"I'm not going home. I'm hitting the town tonight, although the nightlife here is extremely lacking."

"Oh, so you're going on a date tonight?" I pretended to study the menu so I wouldn't have to look at her. "It's just that it's so late. . . ."

"It's only eleven o'clock. And I wouldn't call it dating—it's nothing that formal. Frank and I are just going to . . . *hang out* for a while."

I squeezed my hands into fists, allowing my fingernails to cut into my palms. I liked the word *dating* so much better.

She went behind the counter. "Where do you usually take girls when you go out?"

I laughed. "I'm the last person you should ask about going out."

She looked me up and down, and my pulse jumped into overdrive. "A nice guy like you doesn't have a girlfriend?"

"Had one. We broke up a few months ago. Actually, it was more like she dumped me." Just saying it out loud made me feel like a fool. "Maybe you remember her. Jennifer Dowling—"

"Jenny Dowling? Really? I never would have pegged her as your type. She was way too quiet. Too meek." Madeline leaned over the counter. "So what happened? Why'd y'all break up?"

I turned away from her. Did she even realize how low that tank top dipped?

"Well, come on," she said. "I don't have all night."

I shoved my hands into my pockets. "She broke up with me because I . . ." Good Lord, I couldn't believe I was saying this. "She broke up with me because I wouldn't have sex with her."

Madeline's face was stuck somewhere between shock and laughter. "She asked you to sleep with her and you said no?"

"Well, it wasn't exactly like that. Jenn decided she wanted to have a more physical relationship. Only problem was, I didn't realize this until after she broke up with me. After she had sex with someone else."

Madeline's face twisted into a full frown. "That's a real shitty thing for someone to do. She should have at least talked to you about it." She circled the counter and planted herself in front of me. "But the real question is, if she had asked, would you have slept with her?"

The scent of vanilla and coffee overpowered me. "I don't—I mean . . ." I backed up a little. "We're Christians. We're supposed to wait until we're married."

"Because Lord forbid what would happen to someone if they decided to have sex before they got married." Madeline waved a finger in my face. "I can only imagine what you think of Jennifer now."

Even though I had her beat in height by almost half a **foot**, it felt like she was towering over me. "I mean, yeah, I'm mad at her, but I don't think Jenn's a horrible person. I just wish she had been honest with me."

"Maybe she tried to talk to you about it. Maybe you just weren't listening." She crossed her arms. "You don't know how hard it is to talk about things like sex with someone so . . . good."

I shook my head. "I'm not as righteous as everyone thinks I am."

"Is that so? Well, Mr. Preacher's Son, let me ask you this: Why do you think it's so wrong to have premarital sex?"

"Well, the church believes—"

"See, this is the same problem you had with the essay. You're regurgitating someone else's opinion." She poked my chest, over my heart. "I'm asking you what *you* feel. In here."

Madeline's repeated jabs made it hard to concentrate. "It—it doesn't matter what I think," I stammered. "The Bible is my moral blueprint. It's what I have to live by."

"What is that—some line you heard from your father?" She jabbed me one last time, then moved away. "For your information, the Bible doesn't even say that premarital sex is wrong. All it talks about is sexual immorality."

"But clearly sexual immorality includes premarital sex."

"Again, why? Because some preacher told you so?" She grabbed a black plastic bin from the counter and began busing one of the nearby tables. "Listen, if you want to say that premarital sex or drinking or cursing—or whatever—is wrong, that's fine by me. But right now, you sound like all the other mindless sheep in the church, willing to follow their pastor anywhere, even if it's off a goddamn cliff."

"First of all, I'm not some mindless sheep. Second, it's

a pastor's *job* to lead parishioners—to help them to interpret the Bible. In the book of Jeremiah—"

"You don't have to quote the verse, Joshua." The way she was throwing plates on top of one another, I was sure one of them was going to break. "All I'm saying is, preachers are just men, just like anyone else. They can make mistakes. They can be wrong."

I paused a few feet away from Madeline. I wanted to be angry, to continue arguing with her, but it wasn't me she was mad at—that much I could tell.

"Madeline, does this have to do with why you stopped going to church? Was your father . . . *wrong* about something?"

"How about wrong about *everything*." She placed another plate in the bin, this time much more softly. "Sorry for yelling at you. I tend to get really riled up sometimes."

"It's okay." I took a step toward her; she took two steps farther away. "Hey, I can stick around a little longer, if you want to talk," I said.

"Not much to talk about."

"Are you sure—"

"I hate to be rude, but I'm going to be late if I don't get this place cleaned up." She walked to the farthest corner of the room. "You'd better go home."

I watched Madeline bus another table. "Um, okay. I guess I'll see you later." The only response I got was the clanking of coffee cups.

I headed toward the door. *Maybe Mom was right. Maybe Madeline wasn't ready to—*

"Joshua," she said, so soft that I almost didn't hear her.

I stopped and turned. She had moved by the window—there was just enough yellow moonlight filtering through that I could catch her face. "I'm really glad you liked the book," she said. "Come by the shop later on this week, and we'll talk more. Okay?"

I nodded. She had invited me back. For tonight, maybe that was good enough.

chapter 5

The last thing I wanted to do was pull myself out of bed the next morning. For the first time in months, I'd gone a full night without dreaming about Jenn.

Unfortunately, my dreams were now frequented by a girl even more unattainable than my ex-girlfriend.

I glanced at the leather-bound Bible sitting on my desk. I hadn't even made it through my nightly prayers before my mind had drifted to thoughts of Madeline. Thoughts of vanilla-scented hair, dark purple lips, and low, throaty moans. Thoughts of her warm, freckled flesh pressed against my skin.

But it wasn't just Madeline's body that I kept thinking

about. I kept playing her words over and over in my head, in cadence to the imaginary jab of her finger into my chest.

Why do you think it's so wrong to have premarital sex?

It was a question I had never really thought about before. Until Madeline asked, I had never *had* to think about it. It was wrong. End of discussion.

But still, even though I knew it was wrong and that I couldn't, wouldn't do it, I found myself starting to wonder: Why *did* I think premarital sex was so wrong? Not that I knew a bunch of teens who were having sex, but I did know a few. And so far, none of them had fallen into a chasm of death and destruction. Most of them were pretty normal. Most of them were like me—except they were having sex and I wasn't.

After my alarm clock went off for the third time, I knew I had to get out of bed if I had any intention of getting to church by the time the service started. I hurriedly showered, dressed, and rushed out the door.

I was still fifteen minutes late by the time I slipped into the sanctuary. Dad flashed me a small smile as one of the white-gloved ushers led me to a pew. Just as I squeezed into a seat beside big-boned Bobby Taylor, my phone vibrated in my coat pocket. I flipped open the phone; I had been text-messaged.

Where r u? MMS

It took a second for the initials to register. *MMS*—Madeline Marie Smith.

My fingers tensed around the phone, my thumbs eager

to reply. I sank lower into my seat and tried to duck behind Mrs. Williams and her peacock-feathered hat.

At church. Call you back later?

I was about to hit Send, but then changed my mind. I erased the last sentence and added a new message.

At church. What's up?

What's up—that sounded cool. More relaxed. That was the type of language I was supposed to be using, right?

Bobby Taylor shifted in his seat and grunted in my direction, but I didn't peel my eyes away from the screen. A few seconds later:

I'm at church 2.

I glanced around the sanctuary. I didn't see her anywhere. I wiped my hands on my slacks, then typed another message.

Where? I don't see you.

I stared at the phone for what seemed like hours, waiting for her to respond. Finally, her reply popped onto the screen.

Outside. U know where.

By this time, Bobby Taylor was about to cough up a lung, he was grunting and clearing his throat so hard. I shut my phone and pushed past him. "Excuse me," I mumbled.

As I stepped out of the pew, I caught Dad's gaze again. But this time, I pretended I didn't see him.

* * *

It had been years since I had gone out there, but I still remembered the way.

70

Past the new asphalt parking lot. Down the dirt path to the old wooden fence.

Except I didn't have to jump over the fence this time. Whole sections of it lay on its side, almost obscured by tall prairie grass.

I had never wanted to run as much as I did right then. But I restrained myself. I didn't want to look too eager. I didn't want to get my hopes up.

The grove was as I remembered it, dark green and over-run with thorny shrubs and dead tree trunks. Brown vines and mysterious-looking splotches covered the old shed.

And just like before, the blackberry bush was there, covered in fruit.

Madeline sat on a weathered yellow blanket to the side of the shed. I wasn't sure how long she had been there, but the blanket looked like it had been purposely showered with dead leaves. Unless I was mistaken, she wore the same clothes she had on yesterday.

"This place hasn't changed at all, has it?" she said as I neared her.

"Mrs. Watson died a few years ago. She willed the land to her son, but I don't think he makes it out here very often."

"She died, huh. Thank God for small miracles."

"Madeline, you can't say–"

"She was a bitch. No one liked her. Not even you." Madeline plucked a stray leaf from her jeans. "What did your dad end up doing to you that night, after he found out we had snuck out of church? Was he angry?"

"No, he wasn't angry at all. He just reminded me that as his son, there were some things I couldn't do."

"He talked to you? That's it? That's all?"

"Yeah." I cautiously approached her, my feet crunching over long-dead leaves. "What did your father do?"

She snorted. "A hell of a lot more than talking."

Although the grove was almost entirely surrounded by trees, a gust of wind somehow found its way through the branches and blew past us. Madeline wrapped her arms around her shoulders.

I took off my suit coat. "Here, take this."

"No, I shouldn't . . . ," she said, but she was already taking the coat. She slipped it over her arms; the sleeves went down to her palms. "Thanks," she said. "I hope your coat doesn't end up smelling like smoke."

I sat down beside her. "You smoke?"

"Not me. Frank." She shot me a crooked grin. "Smoking cigarettes is just about the only thing I don't do."

The wind blew through the trees again, and she pulled the coat tighter around her. I tried not to shake, even though the breeze cut through my shirt like water through a cheese grater. "I guess you're wondering what I'm doing here," she said. "And I guess you're wondering why I'm wearing the same clothes I wore last night."

I shrugged. "I figured you just liked blackberries a lot."

"I wish." She traced a path on the back of her hand, connecting freckle to freckle. "After Frank dropped me off this morning . . ." She paused for a second, maybe because of the way I stiffened up. "After he dropped me off, I felt like talking to someone. I thought about calling you, but it was six o'clock in the morning. And Aunt Gwen was asleep." Madeline tugged at the sleeves of the coat. "So I decided to call Mom. Unfortunately, Dad answered the phone."

"What happened? What did y'all talk about?"

Her gaze floated back to her hands. "Let's just say I'm not his favorite person in the world right now."

I scooted closer to her. Her hair smelled like a mix of smoke and vanilla. "I'm sure he cares about you. You're his daughter."

"You didn't hear what he said."

I reached out and linked Madeline's pinky finger in mine, like I used to when we were kids. Like I used to when she was just Maddie, not this purple-lipped stranger. "Well, I think you're great."

Her finger twitched. "You don't even know me."

"People don't change on the inside." I took her entire hand in mine. "You're still the same girl you used to be five years ago, no matter how much you've grown."

Her face shone in the yellow morning sun. "Thanks, but you shouldn't lie like that. You're a preacher's kid."

"You're a PK as well."

She smiled as she ran her thumb along the inside of my palm. It tickled, but only a little. Then she pulled away from me. "I think you should head back to church." She started to slip out of my coat. "I don't want you to get into trouble."

I placed my hands on her shoulders. "I can stick

around for a little bit longer. What's a few more minutes going to hurt?" I made it a point to avoid catching a glimpse of my watch.

"But . . ." She nibbled on her bottom lip. "Well, maybe for a few more minutes. I kind of like the company."

I helped Madeline reposition the coat on her shoulders. She turned the collar up so that the fabric rested against her cheek.

I liked the way she looked in my coat. It was much too big for her, but she looked safe in the oversized sleeves.

"I was actually surprised when you returned my text message," she said. "I figured you'd have your phone off during service."

"If it had been off, you could have always come into the sanctuary."

"You're kidding, right?" Madeline looked down at her jeans. "Those folks would've chased me out if I had come in wearing this. I'm surprised they didn't try to kick me out last week."

"Madeline, I know we can be a little conservative—"

"Conservative? How about downright mean?" She pointed at me, hard and angry. "You people are quick to ask for forgiveness, but won't think twice about condemning others for the same mistakes." She shook her head. "If I was God, I'd be pretty damn ashamed of how fucked up the church has gotten."

Madeline paused to take a breath. I wanted to argue with her, but honestly, I didn't know where to start. Just like last night, she had gone from playful to fuming in a matter of seconds—and I had no idea why. Did she really think all Christians were that bad?

"Not all of us think like that, you know."

She sighed. "I know." She placed her hand on my arm, close to my elbow. The cold from her fingers seeped through my white cotton shirt, chilling my skin. "I shouldn't have yelled at you last night. You're not . . . you're not like everyone else. And neither is your dad—he actually cares about his congregation."

"But I'm sure your dad—"

"He's an asshole." Her fingers dug into my flesh. "He's got all of Sunset Valley Baptist Church convinced he's damn near the second coming of Christ, but he doesn't give two shits about those people." Any second now, I thought she was going to puncture one of the veins in my arm. "He's a phony, and he's an asshole. A big, fat asshole."

She looked down, like she finally realized it was *my* skin she was digging into. "Sorry about that," she said, removing her hand.

The outline of her hand still showed on my shirtsleeve. "Madeline, what happened between—"

"Let's not talk about my dad, okay? I've wasted too much of my life thinking about him."

I nodded. "You know, my dad has his faults, too. He won't let us start a praise-dance team."

Her lips turned up a little. It wasn't a smile, but it was close. "You're thinking about starting a praise-dance ministry?"

"Well, some of the girls in the youth group want to start a praise-dance team. Dad doesn't think the congregation will go for it."

"He's probably right. But don't give up on the idea. I think it could really work."

I hated to admit it, but I wondered if I had already given up on the idea.

"I tried to get my father to start a praise-dance ministry; I hope you have better success than I did." She placed her hand on mine. "Programs like that may not get people into heaven, but it keeps them out of trouble. At least, it's supposed to keep them out of trouble."

"I'm sure my father would *love* to hear that."

"Just because he doesn't want to hear it doesn't mean you shouldn't say it." She stared at me; the weight of her brown eyes shook me to the very foundations of my soul. "If the girls in your youth group really want to start a praise-dance ministry, you should do it."

"But I—but my dad—"

"Like I said last night, he's just a man, Joshua. Just because he's a preacher doesn't mean he's always right."

I focused on Madeline's face, the way her mouth formed a straight, hard line, neither frowning nor smiling. She seemed so sure of herself. Just like Dad. Just like everyone—except me.

"Don't worry, you'll figure it out," she said as if she was reading my mind. "You just need to think about it some more." Then she sucked in a deep breath and looked up at the trees. "I miss this. The quiet and the beauty. I always felt closer to God out here than I did in any sanctuary." She squeezed my hand, her fingers finally warm. "I could never find any place like this in Virginia."

It was amazing how Madeline could be barreling head-first down one course of thought and then come full stop and start talking about something else.

"It is pretty, isn't it?" I looked up; the pines stretched into forever. "I tried to come out here a few times, but I always felt weird. This was your place. I always felt like I was intruding."

"You never brought Jenn out here?"

I shook my head. "She wouldn't have liked it. She isn't into nature." I stared at Madeline as she leaned back, her face to the sky. I wanted to run my fingers along her cheek, down her neck.

"Frank wouldn't like this place either. Not enough noise."

I couldn't stop looking at her neck. I suddenly wanted to know just how much of her body was covered in freckles.

I took a deep breath. "Maybe you need a new boyfriend. One that'll appreciate things like this."

"First of all, Frank's not my boyfriend. He's just a guy I like hanging out with." She angled her gaze toward the shed—away from me—and slid her hand away from mine. "I don't even like him that much. Intellectualism isn't his strong suit."

My fingers were cold without Madeline's hand on mine. "Then why go out with him?"

She shrugged. "All Frank knows about me is that I'm

eighteen, I live with my aunt, and I work at a coffee shop. He doesn't know that my father pastors the fourth-largest Baptist church in Norfolk. He doesn't know I can quote almost any verse from the Bible. He doesn't know I'd hoped to attend an Ivy League school in the fall." She glanced at me. "To him, I'm just a girl who likes to drink a little beer, watch mindless teen comedies, and fool around."

"Don't you want more?"

"Like what? Clever conversation?" She nudged me with her elbow. "That's what I have you for, right?"

I turned away from her, my jaw stiff. *Clever conversation.* That was all she wanted from me. That was all I was good for.

"You got quiet all of a sudden," she said. "You okay?"

I shrugged in response. Out of the corner of my eye, I could see Madeline staring at me, but I refused to look back at her.

We remained like that for a while, her staring at me and me staring at the back of my hands. *First Jenn, now Madeline. The curse of the good guy strikes again.*

"Hey, I want to tell you something," she said. She pushed my knee, forcing me to turn toward her. Then she repositioned herself in front of me, cross-legged. She brought her warm hands to my face and cupped my cold cheeks.

It would have been so easy for me to lean my face toward hers for a kiss. All I needed was a sign—*any sign.*

Madeline didn't look interested in kissing me, though. Her lips were pursed together, almost in a frown. She didn't start talking until I had locked eyes with her.

"There's nothing wrong with being a good guy, you know." Her blackberry-sweet breath floated across my face and tickled my nose. "Good guys like you don't belong with cynical, bitter bitches like me."

"You're not a . . ." I cleared my throat. "You're not like that."

Madeline laughed. "See, you can't even curse," she said as she patted my cheek. "I know it sucks, always being the good guy while everyone else is doing God-knows-what. But you have to be true to yourself. You're a good, kind person, and there's nothing wrong with that." Then she released my face. "Something tells me I'm going to regret this, but what the hell. Maybe I'll go to that party with you after all."

It took me a second to focus on her words. "You . . . you'll go to the party with me? But I thought . . . but you said—"

"We're friends, right? Friends are allowed to go to parties together." She crossed her arms. "But just to be clear, we're going as *just* friends."

I rolled my eyes. "You don't have to keep saying stuff like that. I get the message."

She tilted her head to the side, making her smile look slightly crooked. "Joshua, when are you going to realize, when I say things like that, I'm not saying it for your benefit. Sometimes I need to remind myself."

chapter 6

By the time I got back to church, the service was over. A few people tried to chat with me, but I was too caught up in my own thoughts to have a decent conversation.

What made Madeline walk away from the church? What had happened to her in the five years since she left Conway? Why did she hate her father so much? I was beginning to worry that he took "spare the rod, spoil the child" a little too literally.

And Lord forbid, maybe Madeline's father *didn't* physically abuse her. Maybe he did something *worse*.

I shuddered and tried to ignore the cold, clammy sensation seeping into my skin. I couldn't focus on this now—

I had a youth group meeting in five minutes, and I still needed to look over my notes.

I headed toward the educational wing of the church, but halfway across the parking lot, Deacon Briggs ambushed me. "Your daddy wants to see you," he said, his eyes fixed on my collar.

I wondered if he could smell her scent on my coat. I could.

"Can you tell him I'll be there in a few minutes? I have a youth group meeting and—"

"Don't think he's in the mood to wait, son." He wrapped his arm around my shoulders and guided me to the church.

Deacon Briggs didn't release his grip until we were at Dad's office. Mrs. O'Neal, the church secretary, pointed to Dad's study. "He's waiting for you," she said. "Go on in."

I took a few deep breaths and slowly cracked open the door. Dad looked up. "Come in, Joshua. And close the door behind you."

I inched into his office. Dad's desk was like him—big, strong, sturdy, unyielding. I sank into the chair across from him and offered up a silent prayer for mercy.

Dad peered at me over the top of his glasses. "I noticed that you skipped out on the service today. Are my sermons that boring?" He might have been making a joke, but he wasn't laughing.

"I'm sorry. I planned to come back in, but I lost track of time and—"

"Do you know how it looks for the pastor's son not only

81

to show up late for service, but then to sneak out a few moments later?" He took his glasses from his nose and placed them on the desk next to a golf-ball-shaped paperweight. "You're my son. You have to set a good example."

I squeezed my hands into fists. "I had a good reason for skipping out. Madeline came to church today."

Dad frowned and sat back. "I didn't see her in the sanctuary."

"Well . . . she didn't quite make it inside."

"You're telling me that she came to church, but she didn't come for the service?"

"She wasn't really dressed appropriately. . . . She got into an argument with her father and . . ." I shook my head. "It's kind of hard to explain."

"Hmm. I see." Dad placed his hands together, his fingertips barely touching. "I still don't see what this has to do with you. Unless I'm mistaken, your mother instructed you to leave her be."

"You were the one who suggested I talk to Madeline in the first place!" I knew my voice was borderline insubordinate, so I tried to tone it down. "You guys can't have it both ways. You can't tell me to try to help her, just for Mom to tell me otherwise."

Dad sighed. "I agree, your mother and I haven't done a very good job of communicating with each other concerning the Madeline situation. However, that doesn't change the fact that two days ago your mother told you to stop seeing Madeline."

"But Dad—"

"Deuteronomy, chapter five, verse sixteen. 'Honor thy mother and father, as the Lord thy God hath commanded thee.'"

"What about the parable of the lost sheep? If a man has a hundred sheep, and one of them has gone astray, does he not leave the ninety-nine on the mountain and search for the one that is lost?" I gripped the wooden arms of the chair. "We can't give up on her."

I braced myself, awaiting Dad's rebuttal. Instead . . . wait a minute. Was he smiling at me?

"You missed a few words, but you got it basically right, although I like the poetry of the King James Version better than the New American Standard."

What the–? I was talking about saving Madeline, and all Dad could do was give me a lecture on the different versions of the Bible. No wonder Madeline walked away from the church.

The grin on Dad's face was only momentary. He leaned forward in his chair, his gaze neither happy nor harsh. "Your mother is concerned that Madeline may have a negative effect on you, but I think you're old enough–strong enough–to handle the pressure." With the way he looked at me, I couldn't turn away. "Do you really think you can bring her back to the church? Do you think she'll recommit to the faith?"

I thought for a second; I wanted to choose my words carefully. I didn't want to lie to Dad, especially here, at church.

"I really think I can save her."

I repeated my words in my head. I didn't think I was

lying. I *could* save her—just not necessarily in the way Dad was thinking.

"I'll be honest; I'm not thrilled with the idea of you and Madeline being friends," Dad said. "But like you, I'm hesitant to give up on her so quickly. No one is beyond saving, no matter what one's father may say."

That clammy sensation from earlier started to spread across my skin again. "Madeline's father was pretty strict, wasn't he?"

Dad nodded. "Greg believes his children should mind their manners and respect their elders, and when they don't, he believes they should be punished," he said. "But I don't think he ever crossed the line, if that's what you're suggesting."

I stared at the floor, a sour taste at the back of my throat. "What if he did . . . more? Maybe something worse than physical abuse."

Instead of replying, Dad stood from his desk and picked up one of the golf clubs leaning against the wall. He lined up at an invisible tee and took swing after swing.

I just sat there and watched him. This was what Dad always did when he was thinking.

Dad finally paused, leaning heavily against the club. "I've known Gregory Smith for almost fifteen years, and I've never even remotely seen or heard evidence of him abusing his kids—either physically or sexually."

I rose from my seat. "But just because you didn't see it doesn't mean he didn't do it. And that would explain why Madeline hates him so much."

"A lot of things would explain why Madeline dislikes her father." Dad sighed. "But I'll make a few calls, if it'll make you feel better."

"Thanks. That would make me feel better."

Dad returned to his imaginary golf game, and after a few minutes of silence, I figured Dad was probably done talking. I headed to the door, and just as I opened it, Dad said, "And Joshua, don't ever disobey your mother again. You'll find that she—and I—can be a lot less forgiving."

I turned around and nodded. "Dad, I'm sorry."

"No need to apologize. Just don't do it again." He returned to his golf swing. "You'd better head to your meeting. You're already running late."

Meeting? What was he—*the youth group meeting!*

I rushed out of his office. I couldn't believe I had forgotten about the meeting. I was the one who'd scheduled it.

Mrs. Anderson smirked at me as I entered the library. "There you are," she said. "For a second, I was beginning to think you had forgotten about us."

I just smiled as I made my way to the front of the room. Mrs. Anderson had been filling in as our advisor for the past year, ever since Reverend Lloyd, our old youth pastor, took a position at one of the megachurches in Atlanta. Mrs. Anderson wasn't exactly teen-friendly, but she let us run the meetings and plan our own events, so long as we didn't try to do anything too unusual.

Although everyone between the ages of thirteen and eighteen was considered a member of the youth group, only about twenty of us—well, nineteen without Jenn—were regular members. I had been the president for the last two years.

Before I could even call the meeting to order, Rachel's hand shot up. "I want to add something to the agenda," she said, not waiting for me to recognize her.

"And I told her we were not going to waste time discussing an issue we already voted on," Donna said. Donna was the vice president of the youth group and her twin sister, Dora, was the secretary. You'd be hard-pressed to find a more prim and proper set of twins.

I motioned for Rachel to come forward. Donna and Dora invited themselves to the front of the room as well.

"Why can't we have a revote about the praise-dance team?" Rachel asked. Her once-pink eyelids were now baby blue. "The only reason it didn't pass the first time was because the twins bullied everyone into voting against it."

Donna sighed. "I've tried explaining this to you numerous times, Rachel, but you refuse to listen. You were on the losing end of the vote. You can't bring it up again."

"But that's not fair—"

"No, but it's correct," I said. I could see the twins smiling smugly. "However, someone from the winning side of the vote *can* bring it back up for a revote."

Rachel's eyes lit up. "Good. I'll tell Cassandra to—"

"Hold on," I said. "I don't want to talk about this today—not during the meeting. We have too many other issues to discuss." I patted her shoulder. "But if you want to discuss this after the meeting, we can do it then. Okay?"

Rachel's eyes dimmed a little. "Okay, I guess."

"Good." I smiled at her, but she didn't smile back. She headed to her seat, pausing to mouth something to a handful of the girls sitting around her. They nodded in agreement with whatever she said, all the while cutting their eyes at Donna and Dora. The twins just stared straight ahead, their hands folded neatly in their laps.

I called the meeting to order and after briefly discussing the upcoming retreat, I moved on to the Youth Revival. We still had a lot of planning to do for it, although it seemed like except for Donna and Dora, the group was more interested in picking our social events than reviewing the worship service program. Rachel, usually quick to offer suggestions, spent most of the meeting jotting things down in a notebook. Every time she looked up and caught me staring at her, I looked away.

Finally, after doling out a few responsibilities, I adjourned the meeting. Immediately, Rachel marched to the front of the library. Four other girls, all friends of hers, followed.

Dora remained in the front of the room with me, while Donna talked with Mrs. Anderson. She nodded at whatever Donna said before pushing herself out of her seat and walking out of the room.

Apparently, Mrs. Anderson didn't need to stick around to squash this latest uprising. That was what she had the twins for.

Or maybe, that was what she had me for.

Rachel planted her bony hands on her bony hips. "Will

someone please explain to me—to us—why we can't have a praise-dance ministry?" Her words were loud and charged, and aimed at Dora. "Just because some people can't dance doesn't mean everyone should be punished."

Dora brought her hand to her collar and took a step backward. "If you're looking for something to do, why don't you join the choir like everyone else?"

"Not all of us can sing," Rachel said. "And no offense, but some of us don't want to sing the same old has-been spirituals week after week."

Dora sucked in her breath. "I can't believe you just—"

"And if the boys can have a basketball team, the girls should be able to have a praise-dance team," Cassandra chimed in. "Rachel told us all about her praise-dance team at her old church." The girls nodded in agreement.

"Church is a place of worship, not a dance club," Donna said, joining us in the front of the room. While the Wesley twins were identical, Donna was clearly the alpha female of the pair. "I can't speak for everyone, but I know *some* of us are too dignified to participate in such ungodly activities."

"*Ungodly?*" Rachel moved toward the twins. "Who are y'all to say what is and isn't godly?"

Donna puffed out her chest. "Everyone knows that dancing—especially hip-hop dancing—has nothing to do with God, and everything to do with sex." She reached for her Bible. "It clearly states—"

"Okay, that's enough," I said, stepping in between Rachel and Donna. "Let's all calm down for a second."

As Rachel took a few deep breaths, I thought about how her words reminded me of Madeline's. Same fire, same passion. Rachel knew she was right, despite what I or the twins or anyone else said. Just like Madeline.

I looked at the mob of girls behind Rachel. It seemed like all of them had recently taken to wearing makeup. "I assume all of y'all want to start a praise-dance team."

Four heads nodded. Five, including Rachel's.

I crossed my arms. "And how many of y'all know how to dance—and I'm not talking about the type of dancing they do in music videos."

Elizabeth, who was more round than tall, stepped forward. "What's wrong with hip-hop dancing?" she asked. "On TV, praise-dance teams do hip-hop all the time."

Donna snorted. "You don't honestly believe Pastor Wynn is going to allow hip-hop dancing in his church, do you? Please tell me you're not that naive."

I expected Rachel to lash out at Donna, but instead she turned her gaze on me. "We could learn how to do other types of dance, Joshua." Her voice was so low I could barely hear her. "We'd just have to practice a lot."

A lump formed in my throat as I struggled to say the words I knew she didn't want to hear. "Even if you guys danced something as traditional as ballet, it'd be tough to convince the church to start a praise-dance team when only five girls are interested."

"If you really pushed for a group, we'd have more interest." She placed her hand on my arm, right where

Madeline had earlier applied her death grip. "If you really supported it, the youth group would follow you. We always do."

Rachel's words tugged at my conscience. She wasn't arguing her case, nor was she demanding anything. Not anymore. She was merely asking me to do what I knew was right. She was merely asking me to help her.

I pulled away. "I'm sorry, but the church isn't ready for a dance ministry. We're way too conservative for something so radical."

Her eyes pleaded with me. "If you keep thinking like that, we're always going to be an old, boring church."

"Give it a little more time, okay?" I turned to the other girls in the group. While their expressions were as sad as Rachel's, they were a lot easier to focus on. "I promise, I'll keep talking to my dad about it. Maybe next year."

Donna tucked her Bible under her arm. "I'm glad this is settled. Now we can get on to more important things." She smirked at the girls. "And in case any of you are interested, choir practice starts at seven o'clock sharp on Tuesday nights."

The girls glared back at the twins. It was safe to assume that their thoughts were anything but godly at that point.

As the girls filed out of the room, I sat down at the table and scribbled a few notes on the back of a program. As usual, Dora had been too busy arguing to take minutes.

I finished jotting down my notes and looked back up. I wasn't surprised to see Rachel sitting in one of the chairs, her arms crossed, her gaze stone-cold.

"This isn't fair," she said. "You know it isn't fair."

I rose from my seat and stuffed the notes into my jacket pocket. "What do you want me to say, Rachel? My dad doesn't think we're ready."

"That's a bunch of crap and you know it!"

"Don't yell," I said. "I'm doing the best I can."

Rachel walked over to me. "Be honest," she said, her voice slightly softer. "Do you think we should form a praise-dance ministry or not?"

Yeah, Judas, what do you think?

I leaned against the table. "You know what I think? I think, for once, it would be great if you and the twins and Mrs. Anderson and even my father could agree on something. I think it would be great not to be always caught in the middle." I shook my head. I'd take the giggling Rachel over this one any day.

"I want to give you your praise-dance ministry. But I'm not a miracle worker. Things like this don't happen in a day." I loosened my tie, and finally felt like I could breathe. "I'm on your side, Rachel, but you've got to be more patient. Right now, Dad *hates* the idea of forming a praise-dance ministry."

Rachel's gaze lost some of its hard edge. "Do you think he'll ever change his mind?"

I thought for a second. "I honestly don't know," I replied. "But I'll keep trying." I spit on my palms, rubbed them together, then crossed my heart. "I promise. I'll keep trying."

Rachel's face broke into a smile. "Joshua, what did you just do?"

I looked down at my hands. "Sorry. It's an old thing I used to do with a friend when I was making a promise."

Rachel sighed. "I'll . . . try to be more patient," she said. "But keeping quiet isn't something I'm good at."

"Just give me a little more time, okay? I'm going to work on Dad more. It's just . . . complicated."

The youth group, my parents, Madeline—it seemed like everything was complicated.

"So what happened to you during service?" she asked. "I saw you sneak out, but you never came back in."

"Something came up. I needed to talk to someone." I started to walk out of the room, but Rachel jumped in front of me.

"What's her name?" she asked.

"What . . . what makes you think it's a she?"

"First of all, you're starting to get jumpy." She nodded toward my collar. "Plus you have makeup on your coat. Looks like foundation."

I glanced at my lapel. Sure enough, blotches of brown decorated my collar.

"Her name is Madeline."

"The girl Tony was going gaga over the other day?" Rachel kept her gaze on the makeup stain. "So what—is she your girlfriend or something?"

"She isn't my type."

Rachel looked up at me with big, doelike eyes swimming in sky blue eye shadow. "And what is your type?" she asked, before biting her thumb.

"I wish I knew." I rustled the top of her hair, which I knew she had always hated. "When I figure it out, I'll let you know."

chapter 7

A few days later, on my way to the nursing home, I stopped by the coffee shop.

Correction: I had actually stopped by the coffee shop every day for the past four days, but each time I popped in, Madeline wasn't working. I should have just called her, but as I've said before, I'm not that brave.

Today, she stood behind the counter, mixing up some frothy-looking drink in one of the stainless steel machines. She smiled in my direction, but didn't say anything until she finished serving the customer in front of me.

"Hey, Joshua." She sniffed the air. "You smell like soap. You took a shower just to see me?"

Yes. No. Maybe. I don't know.

I shrugged. "I played a game of hoops with Tony. I won. I showered."

"And for a second, I thought I was special." She winked. "So what can I get you?"

I looked at the menu, even though I knew exactly what I wanted. "Do you have any of that coffee you made last week? The light stuff?"

"Sorry, that was just a special for that day." She looked around quickly, then leaned over the counter. "But wait about ten minutes. I'll brew you a cup after Yvonne's left."

With the way Madeline leaned over, I was glad she wasn't wearing one of those low-cut tank tops. "I don't want to get you into any trouble. . . ."

"It's no trouble." She patted my hand; her fingers sported a thick, shiny new coat of nail polish. "I'm glad you came by. I was starting to miss you."

I smiled, but quickly forced myself to stop thinking about her like that, forced myself to stop reading into her words. No matter how much she smiled at me, she was just a friend. *We* were just friends. She couldn't have been clearer if she had carved it into a stone tablet.

We chatted for a few minutes, but then the coffee shop got busy. I moved to a nearby table and picked up a discarded copy of the newspaper, but I found myself staring at Madeline more than the paper. She greeted every customer with a smile. She danced behind the counter like it was a stage, and she was the center of attention.

As much as I watched Madeline, I also watched the customers, especially the male ones. It was impossible not to notice how their gazes floated a little to the south as they placed their orders. How the men in navy blue power suits and dark red ties seemed to always find a way to make contact with Madeline's hand as they handed her their money. How all the college-aged guys, in their wrinkled T-shirts, black horn-rimmed glasses, and leather sandals, would rave about being in some local band I had never heard of, and would invite Madeline to drop by to check out one of their sets.

Madeline just smiled through every transaction. Her tip jar looked like it wanted to explode.

Once the rush died down, Madeline waved me over to the counter, and like a puppy, I happily trotted back to her.

"Here's your coffee," she said. "I even added sugar and cream, just like you like it."

I took a sip of my drink. I could really get used to this stuff. "So when do you get off?"

"In about five minutes." She dumped a few plates into the sink. "Aunt Gwen is coming to pick me up after she gets off from work."

I readjusted my grip on my cup. "Why don't you let me take you home?"

Madeline paused, her back to me. I could see the outline of her bra strap against her shirt. "You sure you don't mind?" she asked.

Of course I didn't mind. I'd kill to have Madeline all to myself, even if we were separated by thousands of years of experience. "I'd be happy to take you home, as long as you're okay with me making a quick stop first."

"Not a problem. I just need to be home in enough time to change and scarf down dinner before Frank picks me up."

Frank. Her nonfriend who she did nonfriend things with.

"Another night on the town?" My words were more bitter than the coffee.

"I wish. I'm going to hang out with Frank and his crew at the bowling alley. I hate it—all the smoke and all the noise—but it's what Frank loves to do. He plays in a league twice a week."

I placed my cup on the counter. "Can't you suggest something better to do? Something you both like?"

"Like I said before, we don't have that much in common."

I crossed my arms and pinched my sides hard enough to leave a bruise.

Madeline disappeared into the back and emerged a few minutes later with her book bag slung over her shoulder. "So where do you have to stop before you drop me off at home? Just don't tell me it's church, because—"

"It's not Mount Calvary." I grinned at her; it was finally my turn to be a little mysterious. "Don't worry, you'll like it. Trust me."

Madeline arched an eyebrow. "Joshua, what exactly do you have in mind?"

I smiled even more. "How do you feel about old people?"

"I can't believe I let you talk me into this," Madeline said as we pulled up to the nursing home.

"What's wrong with going to a nursing home? I really like hanging out here." I grabbed a plastic bag filled with old magazines from the backseat, and caught a whiff of Madeline's vanilla-and-coffee-bean scent.

She laughed. "No one your age should ever say something like that."

"We don't have to stay long," I said as we entered the building. "I just need to check in on some of the guys, to make sure they're okay. I'll have you home in plenty of time to get ready for your big night at the bowling alley."

"Not funny."

After signing in at the front desk, we headed to the rec room. As usual, Leonard and Mr. Rollins were engaged in a chess game. I didn't have to ask who was winning; I could tell by the grimace on Mr. Rollins's face.

"Whatcha got in the bag, Joshua?" Leonard asked as we approached their table.

"Just some magazines. I figured you guys could use some good reading material."

"Forget the magazines," Mr. Rollins said. "Who's the little lady you brought with you?"

Madeline extended her hand to Mr. Rollins. "Madeline Smith. Nice to meet you."

Mr. Rollins yanked his hat from his head before shaking Madeline's hand. "Carl Rollins." He nodded toward Leonard. "This is my cousin, Leonard King."

Madeline and I sat down at the table. "How have you guys been doing?" I asked.

"Not so well," Leonard said. "Rollins has been coughing an awful lot lately."

"Speak for yourself." Mr. Rollins winked at Madeline. "I feel great."

Mr. Rollins may have felt great, but he didn't sound like it. His voice sounded like he had smoked a thousand cigarettes in a single afternoon.

"This is the first time Carl's been out of his room all week," Ms. Beatrice said as she waddled over to us. She stopped when she reached the table. "Maddie Smith?"

Madeline squinted at the woman before smiling. "Ms. Beatrice?"

"Girl, I remember you when you could barely reach up to my waist. Now look at you." She pulled Madeline from her seat. "Hmm, you sho' did turn out okay."

"You can say that again," Mr. Rollins mumbled.

Ms. Beatrice swatted Mr. Rollins's arm. "Shut up, you old fool. I used to be Maddie's nanny. She was the smartest girl I ever raised. Could read before most other children could even talk." She looked Madeline up and down. "She was just the sweetest little thing I'd ever set my eyes on."

Madeline looked down at her feet. "Thank you."

Ms. Beatrice pulled Madeline into her chest. "Girl, I am so proud of you."

"Stop embarrassing the girl," Leonard said. "You got her turning colors and everything."

Sure enough, Madeline's face had taken on a reddish

purple hue. If it had been a little darker, it would have perfectly matched her lips.

* * *

Once we were back in the car, and once Madeline's face had regained its normal brown color, she said, "It was good seeing Ms. Beatrice. She hasn't changed a bit."

"She seems very fond of you."

Madeline shook her head. "I don't know why she said all that stuff. She doesn't even know me anymore."

"To some people, you're always going to be sweet, innocent Maddie Smith."

Madeline shrugged. "Yeah. To some people."

chapter 8

Studying myself in the mirror for the hundredth time, I reminded myself that I wasn't doing anything wrong. I was taking a friend to a party. Not a girlfriend—just a friend.

So being that this wasn't an official date with an official girlfriend, I figured there was no point in bringing it up with Mom and Dad. They would just make a big deal out of nothing.

The way I saw it, I was doing them a favor.

I entered the kitchen, where my parents were doing their best to pretend they weren't waiting on me. "You look nice," Mom said. "Don't forget Charlotte's present."

"I left it in the car. And don't worry, I got it gift-wrapped."

"Who's chaperoning this party again?" Mom asked. "I know Charles and Gladys won't be there."

I wiped my forehead. "Um . . . I'm not sure. . . ."

"Lily, leave the boy alone." Dad glanced over the top of a Golfsmith catalog. "Have a good time, Joshua."

I started toward the door, but Mom blocked my path. "Are you sure you don't want to eat before you leave?" The top of her head was level with the bottom of my chin. "They never have enough food at those parties."

"Lily!" Dad dropped his catalog and laughed. "Let the boy be."

Mom smirked back at my father. "He's a growing boy. He needs to eat."

With the way my stomach was knotted up, I couldn't have eaten if I had wanted to. "Really, I'm not hungry." I leaned over and pecked Mom on the cheek. "Plus, I really need to get out of here."

"What's the rush?" Mom winked at me. "You don't have some secret date you're not telling us about, do you?"

Mom and Dad laughed. I didn't.

"I'd better go." I stumbled toward the door, my feet heavy. "I'll see you guys tonight."

It isn't a date. Madeline said so herself.

"Have a good time, honey," Mom said. "Don't stay out too late."

* * *

My stomach was still in knots when I arrived at Madeline's aunt's house. I rang the doorbell, and Ms. Smith opened the door. "Come in, Joshua. Madeline should be ready in a few minutes."

Ms. Smith left me in the den while she went to get Madeline. I picked up one of the pictures on the bookcase. It was of Madeline from years ago—tall and skinny, with long black hair and rosy, freckled cheeks. Maybe Madeline didn't want to admit it, but there were times when she still looked a lot like the girl in the picture.

I returned the photo to the bookcase as Madeline entered the room. She placed her hands on her hips and struck a vogue pose. "So, how do I look?"

"Wow" was all I was able to mutter. Her legs stretched for days, from the tips of her toenails to where her thighs disappeared under a crimson sundress. Three earrings sparkled in each ear, and a silver cross dangled from her neck, surrounded by a sea of brown skin.

Madeline spun in place, causing the dress to billow slightly around her. "Like it?"

I nodded. The dress wasn't necessarily tight, but it molded itself around every beautiful curve of Madeline's beautiful body.

She turned to her aunt, who had followed her into the room. "I forgot to charge my cell phone, so I'll probably have it off, to save juice. I've left Joshua's number on the fridge, if you need to get ahold of me."

"Great. That means Frank'll be calling here all—" Ms. Smith caught herself and looked at me. "I'm sorry. I shouldn't be bringing this up."

"It's okay. Madeline and I are just friends." I smiled so

wide the corners of my mouth hurt. "I've heard all about Frank."

"Then you know more about him than I do." Ms. Smith shook her head. "Y'all have a good time tonight."

Madeline grabbed her matching red purse from the couch. "You're not going to ask me what time I'm coming home?"

"You're going out with Joshua," Ms. Smith said. "I don't have to ask."

Madeline kissed her aunt on the cheek, and we left the house. I stopped Madeline before she could step off the porch. She smelled like vanilla and honeydew and every other sweet scent God ever created.

"Are you sure this is okay?" I asked. "I don't want to make Frank jealous."

I hadn't wanted to ask about Frank, mainly because of my urge to projectile-vomit every time I heard his name. I was hoping they'd break up soon. But how do people who aren't even an official couple break up?

Madeline readjusted her purse strap on her shoulder. "No offense, but you're not the type of guy Frank would get jealous over."

Ouch. She might as well have kneed me in my crotch.

Madeline brought her hand to her mouth. "I'm sorry, that didn't come out right. It's just, you're such a good guy. . . ."

I waved her off and tried to put on a brave face. "It's okay. You're not the first girl who's said something like that to me."

"The ex-girlfriend, right?" Madeline sauntered toward

me with a seductive sway. "Want to make her jealous? I'm really good at it."

Madeline's chest was literally millimeters away from my body. One light puff of wind was all it'd take for her to brush up against me.

Does she even realize what she's doing to me? Why am I putting myself through this?

I stepped away from her, trying to keep what little sanity I had. "As much as I'd like to, I don't think it'd be honest for you to pretend you like me when you really don't."

"Who said I'd be pretending?" And then, very quickly, she winked at me.

But then again, maybe she just had dirt in her eye.

* * *

I had washed the car earlier that day, but now Madeline's sweet scent overtook the pine-scented air freshener I had sprayed all over the seats. I focused my gaze on the road, and tried not to become distracted by how Madeline's dress slowly inched up her thighs.

Madeline didn't talk much during the ride; she spent most of the time playing with her necklace or fiddling with the radio. After flipping through a few stations, she settled on oldies.

"I love the old stuff," she said as Marvin Gaye wailed through the speakers. "It's so much better than most of the new crap they play nowadays."

About halfway through the song, my phone rang. Tony sure did know how to pick his moments. Reluctantly, I answered.

"Josh, where are you?" he yelled into the phone. I could hear music—the new crap that Madeline had just put down—blasting in the background.

"We're on our way now."

"I need you to stop by the store and pick up something for me." The music immediately faded away; Tony must have found a quiet room.

I switched hands so I could flip on the signal light. "Sure, what do you need?"

"Condoms."

I was expecting him to ask me to pick up a bag of ice, not a pack of Trojans. I glanced at Madeline out of the corner of my eye. "And, um, what exactly do you need those for?"

"Take a wild guess."

"Tony . . ."

"I swear, if I'd known I'd be needing them, I would have gotten them myself. Charlotte sprang all this on me just a few minutes ago."

"This is her idea?"

"Yeah. Am I lucky or what?" He paused for a second as the music got louder. "I'll be there in a second," he yelled to someone. "Shut the door behind you."

The music grew quiet again. "I'd go get them myself," he continued, "but I didn't drive."

I glanced at Madeline again. "Tony, this really isn't a good time."

There was an angry pause. "For once, can you stop acting like a total choirboy and pretend to be my friend? I'd do the same for you."

Tony *was* right, he'd do the same for me, although I seriously doubted I'd ever need to depend on him for condoms. "Okay. Fine. Just tell me what brand you want me to get."

He was silent for a few seconds. "I don't know. I've never bought condoms before."

"Like I have?"

"Just get some Trojans. Or better yet, why don't you ask Madeline? Knowing her, she probably has some in her purse."

I sighed. "Good-bye, Tony. I'll figure something out." I hung up before he could say anything else.

Madeline turned to me with a curious expression. "Everything okay?"

I tucked my phone back into my pocket. "I need to stop by the store on the way to the party," I said, trying to keep my voice normal.

"What do you need?"

"Um . . . I want to pick up a pack of gum."

"I've got some Big Red," she said as she opened her purse. I thought about leaning over to take a quick peek inside, to see if she was actually carrying condoms, but before I could, she had already found the gum. She pulled out a piece and offered it to me.

I popped it into my mouth. "Thanks." As the strong, hot cinnamon flavor settled around my tongue, I noticed a convenience store to my left. Without even tapping the brakes, I swerved into the parking lot.

"Hey!" she yelled as she banged against the door. "How about a little warning?"

"Sorry." I pulled up to the front of the store. "I want to grab a bottle of water. My throat's kind of dry."

"Don't you think there'll be water at the party?"

I shrugged. "Better safe than sorry."

"Okaaay." She opened her door. "Guess I'll grab something, too."

"No!" I yelled. "I mean, don't get out. I'll get you something—whatever you want."

She settled into her seat. "Joshua, is something wrong?"

"No, nothing at all. There's just no point in both of us getting out. That's all."

She slowly closed the door. "Well, do me a favor and grab me a Diet Coke."

"Be back in a second." I couldn't get out of my car fast enough.

I rushed into the store. Thankfully, the only person inside was the attendant, an older woman with sandy blond hair and heavy black mascara.

I slowly headed toward the coolers, doing my best to discreetly peruse the aisles. Hormel Chili, NyQuil, SpaghettiOs—this place sold everything *but* condoms.

I grabbed a Diet Coke and a bottle of water, and headed up another aisle. Still no condoms. I moved to another aisle.

"Need help with anything, sweetie?" the attendant asked after I had reached my third aisle. Her voice sounded bored.

"No thanks," I said. Then I snapped my fingers, as if I

108

had finally found what I was looking for, and picked up . . . a quart of motor oil.

I continued around the store, looking and lingering. If I felt like I had stayed in one section for too long, I picked something else up. By the time I had made a complete loop around the store, I had added toothpaste, pliers, and a loaf of bread to my collection.

The attendant cleared her throat as I passed by the front counter. "If you're looking for the travel packets of medicine, we keep those up here."

Of course, I wasn't looking for medicine (although I had the feeling I'd be in desperate need of Pepto before the night was over), but I looked behind her. And there, in between the Marlboro Lights and Sudafed, sat the condom display.

God wasn't going to make this easy for me.

I shuffled up to her and tossed my items onto the counter. She arched an eyebrow as she began to ring me up, but didn't say anything.

Finally, she swiped the last item and punched a few buttons on the register. "This it, sweetie?"

The moment of truth. Not looking at the woman, I nodded vaguely at the rack behind her. "I'd like a pack of . . . condoms," I said. Only my words came out more like: *I'd like a pack of . . . kudms.*

"What did you say?" She leaned over the counter. "If you want cigarettes, you're going to have to show me some ID."

"No, not cigarettes." My voice seemed to echo throughout the store. "Condoms."

She turned around and faced the display. "Which ones you want, sweetie? We got extra-large, extra-thin, lubricated, ribbed, studded . . ."

Studded? In my head, all I could see was a condom with a bunch of metal spikes attached to it. "Uh . . . the lubricated is fine."

She grabbed a box and swiped it over the sensor. "We have to keep 'em back here, on account of all these damn teenagers. If they ain't trying to buy beer, they're stealing condoms."

After handing over my money, I glanced at the condom box as she piled it on top of the other stuff: *Latex Luve.* According to the small type, it was guaranteed to provide your partner with soul-shaking, lip-quivering, skin-tingling orgasms—or you could get your money back.

The woman gave me my change, then pulled a very plastic (i.e., clear, transparent, see-through) bag from underneath the counter.

"By any chance do you have paper bags?"

She smiled as she replaced the plastic bag with a paper one. After placing all the items in the bag, she handed it over to me. "Have fun."

I thanked her and rushed out of the store. I probably didn't take a breath between the counter and the car.

"What took you so long?" Madeline glanced at the bag. "What were you doing in there—grocery shopping?"

"Sorry." I pulled out our drinks, then crumpled the top of the bag and shoved it into the backseat.

"What's in the bag?"

"Nothing." I unscrewed the cap off my water and downed half the bottle.

Madeline eyed the bag, but didn't say anything as I backed out of the parking spot. Then, as soon as I put the car into drive, she twisted around and dove toward the backseat.

I slammed on the brakes. "No! Don't look in–" I started, but it was too late. She had already opened the bag.

She smirked as she pulled out the condoms. "I mean, I know I have a bad reputation, but isn't this a *tad* bit presumptuous?"

I felt my face turning into a supernova. "They're not for me. They're for Tony. He and Charlotte are going to . . . well, you know . . ."

"I think it's obvious what they're going to use them for." Madeline dropped the box back into the bag. "I'm just damn curious about what they're going to do with the motor oil and toothpaste."

I tugged at my seat belt. "See, I couldn't find the–"

"That was a joke, Joshua. You're supposed to laugh."

"Oh. Ha ha."

"By the way, good job with picking the lubricated ones. Your friend will thank you for it."

For some reason, that didn't make me feel any better.

chapter 9

When we got to Charlotte's house, cars lined both sides of the street, but I was able to squeeze into a spot a few houses down from hers.

I grabbed Charlotte's gift, and we began our walk up the hilly street to the three-story house. I thought about bringing along Tony's "supplies," but I figured it'd probably be better for him to come out and get them himself.

At some point, Madeline slipped her arm into mine. Her fingers squeezed ever so slightly—hard enough for me to take notice, but not so firm that it hurt.

When we reached the house, I knocked on the door and rang the doorbell, but with the way the music blared, I was sure no one had heard us.

After waiting a few seconds, I opened the door. The party was going full blast. As I dropped Charlotte's present onto the gift table, Madeline asked. "Do you know all these people?"

"No. Most of them are Charlotte's friends from school."

Just then, Tony appeared from around the corner with Hershel Jones, another friend of Charlotte's. "There you are!" Tony yelled. He started to say something else, but after a quick glance at Hershel, he shook his head and closed his mouth.

"Where's Charlotte?" I asked.

Tony pointed upstairs. "Changing clothes. She has four outfits she wants to 'debut' tonight." He took a swig of a red-colored drink. I hoped he was only drinking fruit punch, but I didn't want to ask.

"And who are you?" Hershel asked, his eyes glued to Madeline. Actually, his eyes were glued to her chest.

"Hershel, this is my friend Madeline," I said. "She just moved back to town."

"Nice to meet you," Hershel said to her. "You want a beer or something? I know better than to assume the Boy Scout offered you a drink."

Madeline squeezed my arm again. "I'd better pass on the beer, but I wouldn't mind a soda."

A soda? Had she forgotten about the twenty-ounce Diet Coke she sucked down on the way over here?

Hershel put his hand on Madeline's free arm, a little too close to her chest. "I was just headed to the kitchen."

Madeline glanced at the beer in Hershel's hand before

turning toward me. "I'll be back in a second, okay? This'll give you and Tony a chance to . . . talk."

I watched as Hershel pulled Madeline away. It seemed like every pair of eyes in the room were focused on her as she slipped through the den and disappeared into the kitchen.

Tony stepped closer to me. "You get the stuff?"

"It's in the car, in a brown paper bag in the backseat. I left the door unlocked."

He grinned. "Thanks, man. I knew I could count on you."

"You should just be happy I decided to show up." I rubbed my neck and looked around the room. "Was Rachel ever able to talk your mom into letting her come to the party?"

"There's no way Mom was going to let Rachel come to a house party without chaperones. She barely let me come." Tony shook his head. "It's probably for the best that Rach isn't here. She would have had a fit if she had seen you walking in here with Madeline draped all over your arm."

I frowned. "What does Rachel have against Madeline? She's never even met her."

"You're kidding, right?" Tony chuckled. "Rachel's got a huge crush on you. Haven't you noticed?"

I chewed on the inside of my cheek. *Well, she has been giggling a lot. . . .*

"Y'all would make a good couple," Tony said. "Plus, I trust you more than any other guy she could date."

"But she's only fifteen."

"Charlotte and I were only fifteen when we started dating." Tony shrugged. "Of course, none of this matters, being that you're with Madeline."

"I'm not with Madeline. We're just—"

"Yeah, whatever." Tony started toward the door. "I'm going to get my condoms."

I grabbed his arm, stopping him. "Tony, are you sure you want to do this?"

He shook off my hand. "Josh, stop being such a prude. It's not like this is the end of the world. I'm going to be a senior in high school. I'm using protection. And I'll be losing my virginity to a girl I obviously care about, being that she's been my girlfriend for, like, two years." He shook his head. "I don't know who you've been hanging around with, but as far as high school goes, those are some pretty damn good reasons to have sex." Tony downed the rest of his drink. "There's a bunch of guys from the youth group on the patio. You should go out there and say hello—if you don't feel too holy to talk to us heathens."

I watched Tony march away. He was mad, but I knew he'd get over it—he was Tony.

After he left, I turned and pushed my way through the crowd toward the patio. Charlotte was Catholic, but a lot of her friends went to Mount Calvary, and most were active with the youth group. But no one from the youth group had ever invited me to a birthday bash like this.

I stepped onto the patio and approached the group. "Hey, guys," I said.

Immediately, the conversation stopped and everyone stared at me.

"Wh-what are you doing here?" Lena, our treasurer, stammered, her stubby fingers wrapped tightly around her beer bottle. "I didn't think you were the partying type."

I looked around the group. It was strange, seeing all these people outside of church. Most of the girls showed more skin than newborn babies. And everyone held at least one beer.

"I like a good party as much as anyone else," I said.

They mumbled and nodded, still watching me uncomfortably. James and Scott even tried to shift their beer cans behind their backs.

I sighed. "I really don't care if you guys drink," I finally said.

Lena brought her hand to her chest, covering her half-unbuttoned shirt. "You're not going to tell our parents, are you?"

Who did she think I was, some kind of Christian gestapo? "Of course I won't tell."

Lena exhaled. "Thanks, Joshua." A few of the others smiled.

But still, no one drank. I tried to get a conversation going, bringing up every mundane topic imaginable. And there was plenty of room on the patio furniture for me to sit down, if only they would shift a little in their seats.

No one shifted, though.

Finally, I said good-bye and left the group. As soon as I was a safe distance away, I heard the conversation jump to a roar.

I walked back to the patio door and looked at the group. Was it really that hard for them to be normal when I was around?

"Hey, Joshua."

I froze, my throat suddenly dry. I didn't have to look to see who was standing behind me. I would have known that voice anywhere.

I slowly turned around. "Hey, Jenn."

Jenn had only gotten prettier in the few months since I had last seen her. Her curly, sandy brown hair had grown quite a bit and now reached the tips of her shoulders. Her cheeks had thinned out, making her look older, more mature.

"I figured I'd step outside for a minute, to try to cool down," she said. "But it's hotter out here than it is inside."

I opened the door for her and followed her into the den. We gravitated toward the far corner of the room, as far away from everyone else as we could get. I wasn't sure whether that was a good thing or not.

I gestured to the drink in her hand. "When did you start drinking?"

"Relax. It's just punch." She took a sip. "You know I don't drink alcohol."

I crossed my arms, unsure what to say. I could smell her perfume, but it wasn't a scent I recognized.

While she took another sip of her drink, I scanned the den for Madeline. I finally found her surrounded by Hershel and a bunch of huge, no-neck, football player-type guys. She looked so at ease with them, grinning when they grinned, laughing when they laughed. She looked like she belonged.

"Is that your new girlfriend?"

I turned back to Jenn. She had finished her drink.

"The one in the red," she continued, looking in Madeline's direction. "I saw you walk in with her."

As much as I wanted to, I didn't lie. "Madeline's just an old friend. She's back in town for the summer. You remember her, right? Pastor Smith's daughter."

"That's Maddie Smith?" Her nose crinkled. "Wow. She's changed."

A flash of anger shot through me. "And what does that mean?"

She kept her eyes on Madeline. "She's a preacher's kid. I expected her to dress more conservatively."

"Is that so?" I balled my hands into fists and stuffed them into my pockets. "So I guess preachers' kids are supposed to be the good kids, while everyone else gets to do whatever they want."

Jenn turned her gaze squarely on me but didn't speak for a few seconds. It used to be that I could tell exactly what she was thinking. Now her thoughts were a mystery.

"It was good seeing you, Joshua." She set down her ice-filled glass. "I'd better go. Rodney's probably looking for me."

"So you *did* bring him to the party." I looked around the room, although I had no idea what he looked like. "Why don't you introduce me?"

"I don't . . . Maybe that's not such a good idea."

"Why not?" My heart pounded in my chest, like it always did right before a basketball game. "It'd be rude of me not to meet the guy who's . . ." I paused, breathing hard and fast. "The guy who's *screwing* my ex-girlfriend."

As soon as I said it, I knew it was wrong. Wrong and rude and so unlike the good Christian boy I was supposed to be.

But you know what—forget turning the other cheek. How about an eye for an eye?

Jenn frowned, but not like she was mad. It was more like she felt sorry for me, which made me even angrier. "Even though we aren't a couple, I thought we could be friends," she said. "You could try to be happy for me."

"I am happy. Isn't it obvious?"

Jenn put her hand on my arm. Her touch felt foreign. "You know, there's more to me and Rodney's relationship than sex," she said. "I love him. And I think it's okay to sleep with someone you love."

I shook her arm off. "You can't be serious. You *can't* love him. You've only been dating him for four months."

"Joshua, stop acting like a jerk!" She crossed her arms. "I hate to burst your bubble, but it's your fault we broke up, not mine." Her voice exuded heat. "Do you know how many times I practically threw myself at you?"

For a second, I forgot I was supposed to be mad at her. "What?"

"Remember how often I *conveniently* forgot to wear my bra? Or how about that time I tricked you into coming over to my house when my parents were out of town?" She stepped closer to me. "I wanted more out of our relation-ship. And I know you did too—believe me, I could tell. But you refused to make a move. You refused to take things to the next level." Her words shot daggers into my skin. "It got to the point where I felt like I was dating my little brother instead of my boyfriend. I felt like a slut every time I thought about bringing up sex."

I blinked, trying to bring her words into focus. Madeline was right. Jenn *had* tried to talk to me—to tell me that she wanted to get more physical. I just hadn't listened.

"But you know, it wasn't just the sex stuff that bothered me," she continued. "We couldn't kiss in public because you were worried how it would look. You wouldn't come to my house when my parents weren't home, because you didn't want the neighbors saying anything." She shook her head. "You were more interested in making other people happy—in doing the 'right thing'—than having a girlfriend. You cared more about the church and your parents' opinion than mine—or worse, your own."

I wanted to argue with Jenn, to tell her how wrong she was. But she wasn't wrong. Not at all. Not one bit.

"My father is the senior pastor," I finally said. "There are just some things I can't do—no matter how much I want to."

"I understand that. All I'm saying is, I never felt like I was dating the real you. I never knew what *you* wanted, what you believed. It was always about what the church wanted. What your parents wanted."

"You should have said something. Maybe I could have changed. . . ."

She laughed. "Come on, Joshua. Let's be honest here.

You are who you are." Then she looked thoughtful for a minute. "Actually, that's not fair. Maybe you could have changed. But deep down, I don't know if I wanted you to. Part of me worried that sex would change you—that you'd no longer be one of the good guys. And I didn't want to be responsible for that."

I shook my head. "This is crazy. One minute, you're telling me that you wanted me to be different; the next, you're saying that you wanted me to stay the same?"

She smiled at me—a real, genuine smile. Then she grabbed my hand, and I stiffened. "I wish we had had this conversation earlier," she said. "Maybe things would have been different. Maybe it could have worked out. Maybe—" Jenn quickly released my hand as something behind me caught her eye. "Hey, Rodney."

I spun around, and was immediately face to face with Jenn's giant of a boyfriend.

"Is there a problem here?" he asked. He was so big, his muscles had muscles.

Jenn batted her eyelashes at him. "No problems, Rodney. We were just chatting. Catching up."

"Chatting? Really?" He narrowed his eyes. "It looked like a lot more than that."

I began to back away. "Listen, I was just about to leave."

"Hey, don't run off on my account." He advanced toward me, the red punch in his cup sloshing to and fro. "Clearly, you and my girlfriend have a lot to talk about."

"Rodney, stop it," Jenn demanded. "We were only—"

"There you are," Madeline said, suddenly appearing at my side. "I've been looking all over for you."

Rodney paused as Madeline wrapped her arms around my neck and pushed her body into mine. She leaned her head into me, her lips intimately close to my ear.

"You okay?" Each word she spoke tickled my skin. "Maybe we should get out of here. I'm ready whenever you are."

I nodded. Then Madeline unfolded herself from my body, took my hand, and led me out the door.

chapter 10

"Thanks," I said when we had made it safely to the car.

"I assume that was Jenn, with the way y'all were carrying on," Madeline said. "Her boyfriend was over there
with me, staring you down the entire time."

"Jenn said she loves him." I put the key into the igni-
tion but didn't start the car. "She said it's okay to have sex
with someone if you love them."

Madeline watched me, no doubt waiting for me to continue, but I was too wrapped up in my own throughts to
speak. If Jenn had wanted to sleep with me, did that mean
that she had loved me, too? And had I loved her?

When Jenn and I were dating, I never once uttered the

L word, and neither did she. I liked her a lot, and was sure *one day* I would fall in love with her. But no, I honestly didn't know if I could say that I loved her.

However, that didn't mean she hadn't loved me.

"Maybe she does love him," Madeline said. "Or maybe she just wanted to have sex, and that's how she justified it."

I didn't believe that. I didn't *want* to believe that. Jenn shouldn't have been having sex, but it seemed . . . better if she was sleeping with someone she loved.

"I guess it's not impossible, the idea of her falling in love so quickly," I said. "Stranger things have happened."

"Well I think it's mighty convenient that—" She stopped, and the frown on her face faded away. "You know, it's not important what I think. You're happy and she's happy, and that's all that really matters." Madeline reached over and started the car, and a blast of hot air jetted out of the vents. "You *are* happy, right?" she asked.

I laughed, trying to lighten things up. "Yeah, I'm happy. Especially since I didn't get beat down by Jenn's boyfriend."

"Once Rodney started toward y'all, I figured it might be a good time for us to make our grand exit." She grinned. "Good guys tend not to be the best fighters."

My arms jerked a little as I pulled away from the curb. "I wish people would stop saying things like that. There's more to me than being just a good guy."

Madeline's bright brown eyes drilled through me. "That really bothers you, doesn't it?"

"Sometimes I don't think anybody understands me." I focused on the road and tried to ignore her gaze. "I don't think anyone really understands how it feels to be a preacher's kid."

"*I* understand."

I knew Madeline was being sincere, but I wasn't in the mood to discuss how pathetic my life was. "Sorry for pulling you away from the party. You looked like you were having a good time."

"It's okay. After a while, all the parties are the same. Same dumb guys saying the same stupid things. If anything, I wish I had taken Hershel up on his offer for that beer." She settled into her seat and pulled her purse from the glove compartment. "Did you enjoy the party?"

I thought back to how comfortable everyone else had looked. "I would have had more fun at the nursing home."

"Well, to hell with that lame-ass party." Madeline flipped on my overhead light. "Now where are we going?"

"I assumed I was taking you home."

"Are you kidding? The night hasn't even started yet." She pulled a tube of lipstick and a compact mirror from her purse. "You promised to take me to a party, and I intend to hold you to your word. You're taking me dancing."

"Dancing? You mean, like, at a club?"

"Well, I'm not going to dance in the middle of the street."

"But what about Frank?"

"How many times do I have to tell you—Frank's not my boyfriend."

My fingers choked the steering wheel. "Of course he isn't. Y'all just do *stuff*."

Madeline remained quiet as she applied a fresh coat of lipstick. I knew I should have apologized, but I didn't want to. I was only repeating what she had said herself.

After seconds of painstaking silence, Madeline closed her lipstick and snapped her mirror shut. "Pull over."

"But it's dark. And we're not even close to a side street."

"Pull over. Now."

I gulped, turned on my signal light, and veered onto the shoulder of the road. Cars whizzed past us at an alarming speed, but that didn't stop Madeline from opening her door and marching to the front of the car. She stood with her arms crossed and glared at me until I got out.

"Madeline, I'm sorry," I said before I had even reached her.

"Joshua, I know you're upset and angry and hurt, so I'm giving you a pass." She jabbed her finger into my chest. "But if you ever say anything like that again, I'm gonna stick my foot so far up your ass, you'll be licking my toenail polish off your tonsils for a month." Then she smiled. "Now give me your keys. I'm driving."

Not being one to argue with eighteen-year-old baristas in red sundresses, I handed her the keys and we returned to the car.

Madeline didn't even check the rearview mirror as she pulled back onto the road. "You'd better buckle up." She floored the gas pedal. "I like to drive fast."

*　*　*

"Stay here," Madeline said as we walked up to the edge of the club. "I'll be back in a second."

I stayed in the shadows of what must have been the seediest-looking building in Conway. Broken beer bottles littered the cracked asphalt pavement. There was a tinge of smoke in the air, and I wasn't naive enough to believe it was solely from cigarettes.

Madeline sashayed toward the bouncer. She was tall, especially in her heels, but he towered over her. She beckoned to him with her finger, and he immediately doubled over so that they were face to face. Madeline placed her hand on his shoulder and said something to him. He looked at her for a few long seconds, and finally nodded.

Madeline smiled and waved me over. The bouncer looked even bigger up close—Jenn's boyfriend was a dwarf compared to him. His black T-shirt struggled to contain his biceps. He sported black and brown dreadlocks and an ugly scowl.

"This is my friend Joshua," Madeline told him. "Like I said, he forgot his ID."

The bouncer sneered at me. "Give me your hand."

I extended my sweaty hand to him, palm up. He grabbed it, flipped it over, and plastered a rubber stamp on the back of it. "If I see you with a drink, I'm throwing you both out."

"Yes, sir. No drinks. I promise."

He nodded toward a much smaller guy standing

behind a counter just inside the building. "It's a ten-dollar cover charge."

My hands trembled as I pulled the money from my wallet. I handed the cashier two tens, but he shook his head and handed one of the bills back. "Just ten for you," he said. "Free for her."

Madeline took my stamped hand. "It's usually five for girls, but Patrick and Ross always let me in for free." She winked. "I'm something of a celebrity around here."

Madeline led me inside the main room of the club, which basked in flickering neon lights. The entire room vibrated with every downbeat of the reggae music pumping through the sound system. I was afraid she was going to pull me onto the dance floor. Instead, she led me to a worse location—the bar.

She pushed her way past a couple of guys and leaned against the bar, her chest resting on top of the dark wooden veneer. "Hey, Chris," she said. "Let me have two tequila shots."

I hated the way the bartender leered at her, his dark eyes glued to her chest. Once he turned from her and began to pour the drinks, Madeline smirked at me. I didn't smile back.

"Don't be like that, Joshua." She stood upright again. "I'm trying to get us drinks without having to show ID."

"Maybe you forgot, but I don't drink."

She rolled her eyes. "And I thought you said you were tired of being a saint."

The bartender came back, drinks in hand, eyes on Madeline. She handed him a few bills and took the drinks, a wedge of lime teetering on the rim of each glass. "Come on. It's too crowded over here."

I followed her to the far end of the bar. Madeline removed the lime from one of the glasses, and without even pausing, she downed the shot. Her face scrunched up for a half second before returning to normal. Then she placed the lime in her mouth and sucked long and hard.

At that instant, I knew I would be jealous of limes for the rest of my life.

"Hmmm." Madeline ran her tongue over her lips. "Good stuff."

I wondered just how good those shots were. I mean, if Madeline and the guys from youth group and just about everyone else in Conway could drink, maybe it wasn't that big a deal.

Hey, even Jesus turned water to wine, right?

Maybe Madeline sensed a shift in my thinking, because she nudged the other shot toward me. "You can have it, if you want it," she said, her voice low and throaty and dead sexy. But before I could decide whether to reach for it or not, she pulled it back. "No, you'd better not. Someone has to drive."

Yeah. *Lucky me.*

She knocked back the second shot, and the same pained expression came to her face. "Yuck! I may as well be guzzling gasoline."

"Then why even drink it?"

She placed the shot glass next to the other one, both stained with lipstick. "Because it's fun."

Madeline sat down on one of the stools, and I just

about came unglued with the way she straddled that seat, that dress of hers barely hiding her shiny brown thighs.

"I don't bite." She patted the stool next to her. "You can sit beside me."

I sat down and Madeline took my hand. She laced her fingers through mine and held my hand in her lap. Her red dress scorched my skin.

Madeline swayed in her seat for the next few songs, and I sat there watching her sway, wanting to be pulled along with her.

I could have sat there forever and watched her, but when the DJ played a different, more upbeat type of reggae, Madeline jumped out of her seat. "I love dancehall!" She started toward the dance floor, lugging me behind her. "Come on," she coaxed. "Dazzle me with your greatness."

I was so busy watching her walk, I almost tripped as she weaved through the crowd forming on the dance floor. "I'm not much of a dancer," I yelled over the music.

She stopped in the middle of the floor and placed my sweaty hands on her soft hips. "Just move from side to side. Sway a little."

Maybe it was my imagination, but I swore I could make out a pair of lace underwear beneath her dress, beneath my fingers.

Madeline moved her body, perfectly in tune with the music. I shuffled my feet and tried to do the same, but the song was too fast. I focused on my feet, watching them stumble back and forth, side to side.

After a few seconds of me floundering around, Madeline stopped moving. "You're thinking about it too hard."

I kept staring at my feet. "The music's too fast. I feel like I'm making a fool of myself."

She took my face in her hands and made me look up. "Stop worrying about what other people are thinking. Nobody's looking at you."

I glanced around. It was true—everyone else was too busy grooving to the music to pay attention to me.

"Close your eyes. Listen to the music. Let it take over your body."

I closed my eyes and tried to relax. My feet moved from left to right. My hips swayed in rhythm to the beat of the song. I breathed in the music, letting it pump through me.

I opened my eyes to see Madeline beaming. "Much better," she said.

We continued to dance—if you could call what I was doing dancing—for two songs. Just when I felt like I was gaining control over my rhythmic spazzing, the DJ switched to a slow song with a soft, pulsating beat.

I stopped dancing, unsure what to do with my hands, with my body. "We can sit this one out if you want," I said. "I don't really like slow songs."

She grinned. "What? Don't you want to get close to me?"

"Well, I . . ."

Madeline slid her arms around my neck and leaned into me, and I lost the ability to speak. My arms tightened around her waist, my palms resting on the curve of her bottom. Her scent engulfed me.

"You're a good slow dancer." She laid her head on my shoulder; her body melted into mine. "I like the way you hold me."

I liked the way I held her as well.

* * *

"You're not as bad a dancer as you think you are," Madeline said when we left the dance floor a few songs later. "Your body has a natural rhythm—if you allow it to be taken over by the music."

We headed to one of the booths along the far edge of the club. Madeline hesitated as we passed the bar, but didn't stop.

We slipped into the booth. This time, she didn't have to ask me to sit by her. "How'd you learn to dance like that?" I asked.

"I used to take classes. Dad made me stop, though. He said my movements sent 'mixed messages.'"

"That sounds like something my dad would say."

Madeline shook her head. "Your dad is a good, kind man. He's nothing like my father." Her eyes glowed with sadness. "Let's talk about something else. I don't like getting depressed when I drink."

"Your dad . . ." I stopped, letting my words disappear into the pounding music and flashing lights. Now wasn't the time to discuss her father, but then again, it never seemed like a good time.

What had he done to her? Why didn't she ever want to talk about it?

I just wanted her to talk to me. Then maybe I could

help her. I could show her how beautiful and perfect she really was.

We sat there, friends and strangers at the same time. After a while, an old guy walked by with a container of roses. "Want to buy a rose for the pretty girl?" He looked like he hadn't shaved in years, and he smelled like wet newspaper. "Only three dollars."

I reached for my wallet. "I'll take a red one."

Madeline grabbed my wrist, her fingers sticky and damp. "Joshua, what are you doing?"

With my free hand, I pulled three crisp dollar bills from my wallet. "What do you think?"

"Have you looked at those roses? They look like he pulled them from the bottom of a ditch." She let go of my wrist. "If you really want to buy something, get me another drink, not a rose."

I laughed, even though I knew she wasn't joking.

I handed the guy my money. Maybe he was annoyed at Madeline, or maybe he was upset that I didn't give him a tip, because he bypassed all the decent roses and handed me the most god-awful-looking one, yellow with torn petals and a crooked, thorny stem.

Madeline turned toward the man, who had already moved on. "Hey, what the hell is this supposed to be?" she yelled. "This is a damn rip-off."

"Madeline, calm down." Trying not to prick myself, I gently peeled off the worn outer layers. I held it in front of me to inspect, and sure enough, I caught my thumb on one of the thorns.

"Take it back and get another one," she said. "You deserve better for your money."

I broke off the top three thorns and then broke off the stem below that. I extended the rose to her. "There you go, good as new."

Madeline stared at the flower for a few seconds, her hand hovering in the space between me and her. "Thank you," she said, finally taking the rose. She brought it to her nose and took in its scent. "It's beautiful."

I scooted closer to her so that her thigh pressed against mine. "I don't know what happened between you and your dad, but I think—"

"Shhh." Madeline put her fingers to my mouth. "You know, most guys would have tried to kiss me by this point in the date." She tucked the rose behind her ear and smiled that beautiful smile of hers. "I'm starting to wonder what's taking you so long."

I tried to think of something charming or witty or romantic to say, but instead I just said, "I thought this wasn't a date?"

Madeline paused, her lips floating in front of me. In my head, a big red neon sign flashed: *Stupid, Stupid, Stupid!*

She laughed. "Shut up, you big saint, and kiss me."

And, being the good obedient boy I was, I did.

chapter 11

Although it's not stated as such in the Bible, most people think that lust is one of the seven deadly sins. After that first kiss with Madeline, I had to agree.

As I pulled up to her aunt's house, many hours and kisses later, my whole body hungered for her, quivering and tingling. I turned to her and she obliged, sliding her hand behind my head and pulling me to her face. I tasted the tequila and lime on her lips, on her tongue, but I ignored it. Once you got used to the taste, it wasn't that bad.

After a few minutes, she pulled away and took a breath. "You're quite the kisser, aren't you?"

I shrugged. How was I supposed to answer that?

She took my hand and pecked my fingertips. "I like kissing you," she said. "I like being with you. It's so . . . I don't know. Simple. Easy."

We sat in silence, my hand cradled in hers, her fingers soft against my skin. I watched her—studied her—as she looked out of her window toward the house. None of the lights were on inside.

It's funny, but the more I sat there, taking in Madeline's shape, the more I thought about what Jenn and Tony had said to me earlier that night. To them, I was a saint. A prude. A guy who lived for everyone else, not for himself.

I didn't want to be that guy. Not tonight. Not with Madeline.

But before I could summon the courage to do anything, Madeline released my hand. "I should go." Her breath fogged the window. "Tequila always gives me a hangover in the morning."

"Can't we hang out a little more?" Good Lord, I was practically begging.

"Just being curious, if we did hang out, what would you do? What would *we* do?"

I opened my mouth, but no words came out.

She leaned over and kissed me quickly, saving me from the shame that was no doubt etched on my face. "Come on. It's getting late." She touched her rose, still perched behind her ear. "Plus, I want to get this in some water."

We got out of the car and headed up the steps. I tried not to focus on her body as she swayed in front of me.

She stuck her key into the doorknob, but didn't unlock

the door. "What if . . ." She let her hands fall to her sides, her purse bouncing against her thigh. "What if I called Frank tomorrow and told him I didn't want to see him anymore? Would you be okay with that?"

I nodded, even though she wasn't looking at me. "I'd like that a lot," I said. I fought the urge to say more.

Madeline turned around then, her purple lips beckoning to me in the darkness, and kissed me. I breathed her in, savoring the taste of tequila and lime.

With a light thud, her purse fell to the wooden porch. I slid my hand to her stomach, then around her waist. My fingers ached to touch her.

Madeline pushed herself even further into me; her tongue danced circles with mine. She ran her fingers along the back of my neck. Her thumb pressed hard against the vein throbbing underneath my skin.

A sigh escaped from her lips—or perhaps I was the one who sighed. I wasn't sure anymore; the lines between our bodies and mouths and skin had blurred to the point where I couldn't tell where I ended and Madeline began.

I moved my hand to her face, her cheek sticky and warm. My hand slid lower, and I hesitated for a half second as my fingers brushed against the silver cross hanging from her neck.

I could do this.

I was not a saint.

I was not a prude.

My hand floated lower and lower, until my fingers cupped her breast. I squeezed.

She breathed in hard, and the kissing intensified. I

drowned in the wetness and warmth of her mouth. I pushed against her, sandwiching her between me and the reddish orange brick of her aunt's house.

I squeezed harder, kissed harder. I wanted her so badly. I wanted . . .

Wait.

Something was wrong.

Her hands lay frozen on the back of my neck. Her lips remained still against mine; her breaths were non-existent.

I opened my eyes and she stared back at me, her gaze a mixture of sadness and surprise.

"Joshua . . ." She pushed me away, firmly but not forcefully. "We can't . . . I can't—"

"I'm sorry," I said, retreating from her. "I don't know what came over me—"

"No, it isn't your fault. I shouldn't have led you on." She swooped down and grabbed her purse from the porch. "You'd better go."

"Madeline, I'm so sorry—"

"Joshua." She placed her hand on my chest, her fingernails almost invisible against my black shirt. "I had a really good time tonight. Let's not ruin it, okay?"

I nodded, and she leaned in and gave me another kiss. "Thank you for the rose," she whispered.

She disappeared into the house, and I drove back home. The silence that filled the car did nothing to soothe my guilt.

Madeline had said that I hadn't done anything wrong, but that wasn't true. I had wanted her. *Lusted* after her. I was supposed to be a good guy. A gentleman. A preacher's kid. Instead, I had tried to—actually, I didn't even know what I had been doing. I didn't really want to sleep with her, did I? I just wanted . . . *more*. More than a few passionate kisses. But how much more, I wasn't sure.

Maybe I just wanted her to look at me the same way Charlotte looked at Tony. And she had, for a second. Then I had to go and mess everything up.

By the time I got home, my lower half had relaxed enough to allow me to walk in a somewhat normal fashion, which was a good thing, being that Dad was still awake. He sat at the kitchen table, his Bible open, a white pad full of notes in front of him.

"You have a good time tonight?" he asked, scribbling on his notepad.

"Yeah, it was okay." I tried to make my voice sound as flat as possible.

"Good. I think your mother was starting to get worried, but I reckon that's just her nature." He put his pencil down and looked up. "No mother wants to see . . ."

Dad paused, his eyes narrowing and focusing in on me. Did I look that guilty?

He cleared his throat. "As I was saying, no mother wants to see her baby grow up."

I nodded, unsure how to respond, and inched toward the hallway. "Well, I'm going to bed."

"Joshua." He looked back down at his Bible. "I thought you were supposed to help her recommit to God. I thought you were strong enough . . ."

Dad's voice was so low that it was barely audible, yet it still cut into me like a dull knife. How could he know? How could he possibly know?

I stepped toward him. "Dad–"

"Just go to bed, Joshua." Dad sounded tired. Defeated. "We'll deal with this tomorrow." He flipped a page in his Bible. "And be sure to stop by the bathroom on the way to bed. You look like you were attacked by a box of crayons."

I tried to walk calmly, smoothly, out of the kitchen, but as soon as I was a safe distance away, I flew to the bathroom.

My mouth dropped open as I stared at myself in the mirror. I did look like I had been attacked by crayons.

Purple, lip-shaped crayons.

chapter 12

It was barely six o'clock when Dad opened my bedroom door the next morning. "I'm going to the driving range," he said, his gaze focused on the floor. "Be ready by the time I get back."

Then he shut the door, and a few minutes later, I heard him pulling out of the garage.

If Dad had taken a second to look at me, he would have seen that I was awake and fully dressed. I had spent most of the night tossing and turning, thinking about how I had managed to disappoint both Madeline and my father. I couldn't be the guy either one of them wanted me to be.

Dad returned about an hour later, and we headed to

Bea's Diner for breakfast. We remained silent for most of our meal, with nothing but the occasional clink of our forks against our plates to break the silence. He spent most of his time staring at his plate, but every so often he'd glance at me, the dark circles under his eyes heavy and sad.

"It's not what you think," I finally said.

Dad settled into the cushions on his side of the booth. "So tell me, Joshua, what am I supposed to think? If your son snuck into the house at almost midnight with lipstick smeared across his face, what would you think?"

"I wasn't sneaking into the house."

"Oh, I see. So that makes it better." He took a sip of his coffee, and I did the same. This stuff was crap compared to what Madeline usually served.

"Nothing happened. We just kissed a little." I dumped more sugar into my coffee. "I should have told you and Mom that I was taking Madeline to the party. I'm sorry."

"I'm sure that nothing did happen, but that's not the point. The Bible says to abstain from the *appearance* of all sin. You can't just do what you want to do, whenever you want to do it. You're a role model—not only to the youth in the church, but to the kids at your school, the kids in the community. Even a lot of adults look up to you."

"But I never asked for anyone to look up to me."

"Neither did Moses. Or Abraham," he said. "I know it's not fair, but you have to set the example. The church needs you to be strong. *I* need you to be strong."

Dad had been saying the same thing since I could

walk—how I was called to lead, to be an example of God's glory. But that was easy for Dad to say—he didn't have to pretend to be friends with all these people who supposedly looked up to me. He didn't have to struggle to find things to talk about with the youth group.

"You keep talking about what everyone else needs, but what about Madeline?" I asked. "What about what she needs?"

Dad poured cream into his coffee and slowly stirred. "Over the past few days, I've made a few calls—done some checking up on Madeline's father like you asked. And there's no hint of him abusing her in any way. I also called him this morning and asked him outright. Of course, he denied everything, and was understandably upset when I broached the subject."

"But that doesn't mean he didn't do anything."

Dad drank some coffee. "Did Madeline ever tell you why her father refused to pay her tuition to Brown?"

"He hates her, that's why."

He shook his head. "Madeline got *kicked* out of her prep school. She was caught with a boy and with drugs in her dorm room."

I shifted in my seat. "Everyone makes mistakes—"

"The drugs were in plain sight on her dresser, she and the boy were drunk, and they were . . . in a very compromising position."

Dad might as well have doused me with lighter fluid and set me ablaze. He watched me, looking for a chink in my armor. I did my best to look stoic, but I knew he could see that my insides were crumbling. I just wasn't sure if I was shocked or jealous.

"Why are you telling me this? If anything, this just proves she needs help. And it doesn't mean her father isn't lying!"

"I agree. But you're not in any position to help her."

"But—"

"You need to be realistic." Dad set his mug back down on the table, hard enough for some of the coffee to splash out. "Can you honestly sit there and say that you're not attracted to her? That you don't want to be more than just friends? That you don't want what she's probably very willing to offer?"

I immediately thought back to the warmth of Madeline's lips on mine, the taste of tequila on her tongue.

"I'm not sure what happened to Madeline to cause her to change, but your mother is right," he continued. "She isn't someone you should be associating with. She's dangerous."

"So what? I'm supposed to just stop talking to her? Just like that?"

Dad nodded. "I wish I could tell you something different, but this is bigger than her. Sometimes the needs of the many outweigh the needs of the few."

He pulled his wallet out of his pocket and dropped a few bills onto the table. My plate was still full, but I had long ago lost my appetite.

He patted me on the shoulder as we headed to the car. "I don't think Madeline's beyond salvation," he said. "But you have to trust me and your mother on this. You can't save someone who doesn't want to be saved."

And that was when I knew Dad was wrong. Because when Mom and Dad and everyone else saw Madeline, all they saw was the girl with the bad attitude and sexy body who didn't care about her faith or her family or even herself. The girl who threatened to sway me from the path of the righteous.

But when I saw Madeline, I saw a girl who prayed before every meal. A girl whose eyes shone with sadness every time her father was mentioned. A girl who desperately needed someone to tell her she was good.

I saw a girl who was asking—no, begging—for someone to help her.

"So no more trips to the coffee shop," Dad said as we got into the car. "You'll leave her alone, right?"

I slammed the door shut and looked out the window so he wouldn't have to see me lie. "Right."

*   *   *

Dad dropped me off at home before leaving for a meeting at church. As soon as he disappeared down the street, I jumped into my car and headed in the opposite direction.

I had to talk to Madeline, face to face.

I wanted to tell her how much I liked her and how much I enjoyed hanging out with her last night.

I needed her to see that I wasn't an idiotic jerk who went around groping girls, trying to get them into bed.

She had to understand—it didn't matter what anyone else said or what had happened in her past. She was beautiful and funny and brilliant, and I'd gladly drink all the coffee in Conway if it meant I could see her every day.

But when she opened the door, the words I intended to say got stuck in my throat.

"I hoped it would be you," she said. She shielded her eyes as she looked at me. The sun outside was a floodlight compared to the darkness of the house.

"I know I should have called first. . . ."

"No, it's okay. I was supposed to go into work first thing this morning, but I called in and switched to an afternoon shift. I had too much on my mind; I didn't want to be surrounded by a lot of people."

"If you want, I can come back later."

She shook her head. "I've got to head to work in about an hour. Plus, we have a lot to talk about. That's why you're here, right?"

I nodded as I stepped out of the sunlight and into the house. Madeline led me down a dim hallway and pushed a door open.

"I hope you don't mind talking in my room," she said. "We only keep the air-conditioning on in the rooms back here."

I looked around. "I've never been in a girl's bedroom before."

"I hate this room—especially these bland white walls. It reminds me of a hospital." Madeline gave off a dry, nervous laugh. "I want to paint the room purple, but Aunt Gwen won't let me. Actually, since my dad owns the house, I guess he's the one who won't let me paint." Madeline brought her hand to her mouth and chewed on her thumbnail. Her other fingernails already looked like they had been duly gnawed on.

"I really enjoyed last night," I said.

Madeline stopped chewing on her thumbnail long enough to smile. "Me too," she said. "But I think one date's all we're going to get."

I watched her go back to work on her thumbnail. "Madeline, if this is about the way I acted last night, I'm sorry."

"My mom called me this morning. She told me your dad called my dad to get the skinny on me." She moved her hand away from her mouth. "I heard that you thought I might have been abused."

"It's just . . . you hate your father so much. . . ."

"Don't worry, he didn't do anything wrong. It's not his fault I'm so screwed up." She smirked. "What else did your dad find out about me?"

"Nothing of importance."

"Exodus, chapter sixteen, verse twenty: 'Thou shalt not bear false witness against thy neighbor.'" She swept her bangs to the side of her face. "Your dad told you about how I got kicked out of school, right?"

I nodded.

"Maybe now you'll wise up and stop hanging out with me."

"But Madeline, I don't want to stop seeing you." I walked over to her, the scent of vanilla intensifying with each step. "I mean, I know I'm not like the other guys you've dated."

"And maybe that's what I like about you." She turned away from me and stared at the top of her desk, which was covered in books. The yellow rose I had given her sat in a small plastic cup.

"What are we doing?" She spun back around. "Are you looking for a girlfriend or is this just about sex?"

I held up my hand like I was taking a pledge. "Sex is the farthest thing from my mind."

She rolled her eyes.

"Okay, maybe not the farthest thing." I sat down on the corner of her bed. "I mean, I like kissing you. But I don't want to have sex. I just got carried away last night."

"Joshua, I promise, I didn't let you do anything I didn't want you to do." She smiled, and I knew she was telling the truth. "But you have to realize, if we keep on doing the things we're doing, we're bound to end up having sex."

"I dated Jenn for over a year, and I didn't have sex with her."

Madeline planted her hands on her hips. "And do I look like Jenn?"

Okay, she had me on that one.

She leaned against her desk and stared at her bare feet. "I'm afraid the more you hang around me, the more I'll corrupt you."

"Corrupt me?" I forced myself to laugh. "Please. I'm still the same old Joshua."

"But I'm not the same old Maddie." She took in a big gulp of air, and took even longer breathing it out. "I was fifteen when it happened."

I was almost stupid enough to ask what "it" was, until it dawned on me.

"Dad and I had just gotten into another fight. It all started because he wouldn't let me go to some stupid party that night." She kept her gaze on her feet. "He said that with the way I was built, every boy at the party would be trying to get into my pants."

I thought again about how I had groped her, and I wanted to die. "Your dad was probably right."

"I can't live my life worrying about what other people think about me. If that was the case, I'd never leave my room." Madeline balled her hand into a fist and pounded her palm. "I mean, come on. It was a school dance. He acted like I was joining a harem."

"So you decided to go anyway?"

"Damn right. I went to that party, found my boyfriend, and took off with him. Dad had been accusing me of sleeping with Carlos for months. That night I decided to prove him right."

Now I had to turn away from her. "Madeline . . ."

"Don't worry, it was nice and romantic. His car seats were real leather, not that cheap vinyl that leaves rubber marks on your back." She shrugged. "Anyway, after it all went down, he did what all guys do—he told his friends. And they told their friends. And I got a reputation." She ran her fingers through her hair. "Maybe I started believing all the rumors, because the next thing I knew, I was jumping from boyfriend to boyfriend."

"You don't have to tell me your entire past. I don't

care." I wasn't lying; I really didn't care. I could take Madeline with all her baggage. I just didn't want to know about it.

"I'm only giving you the highlights. This is in no way my entire history," she said. "When Dad finally got fed up with me, he shipped me off to Trinity Christian Academy. That's where I met Jeremy. He was a genius, but he had a little problem with marijuana. And in the process of dating him, I developed a little problem with marijuana as well."

"You became a drug addict?"

"You've been watching too many after-school specials. All I did was smoke a little weed. I never did any of the harsher stuff. I may be reckless, but I'm not an idiot." She sighed. "But then again, you have to be pretty stupid to get caught with drugs, alcohol, and a half-naked boy in your dorm room."

I rose from the bed. "I think I've heard enough."

"But I haven't even gotten to the part about all the lewd sex acts."

"That's not funny." I walked to the opposite side of the room.

"See, this is why we can't be together," she said. "I have a history. A bad history."

"But I can help you—"

"There you go, using your 'thou shalt save the unholy' voice." She hugged herself. "I like me just the way I am."

"That's not how you sounded last night."

"I was drunk. I say a lot of stupid things when I've been drinking."

We stood silent for a few moments, neither of us moving. Madeline chewed on the inside of her cheek while I gritted my teeth. I heard the ticking of her wristwatch all the way across the room.

"You'd better go," she finally said.

"You know, you say that a lot. You're always kicking me out."

"Maybe this time you'll get the point and stay away."

More silence. More ticking. No movement.

"My life is pretty complicated," Madeline said. "I don't need someone swooping in and screwing everything up. I don't need a savior."

"I promise, I'm not trying to force you into going back to church or anything like that," I said. "I just want to be your friend. That's all."

Madeline laughed. "Don't you get it? Girls like me can't be 'just friends' with guys."

"But Madeline—"

"I've got to get ready for work." She opened her bedroom door. "Do you mind letting yourself out?"

I shook my head and headed toward the door. As I passed by her, I paused. "You're a good person, Madeline."

"That depends on your definition of good." She pecked my cheek, then patted it. "Thanks for understanding."

I don't understand, I wanted to scream. But I didn't. I didn't even mumble. I just walked out of her house. I was even sure to lock the door before I closed it.

chapter 13

Madeline haunted my dreams that night. Every time I closed my eyes, I could hear her voice whispering in my ear, telling me all the things a seventeen-year-old wanted to hear. Obviously, they were not the type of dreams God-fearing Christians should be having. But given what Madeline had told me, I didn't have to worry about my dreams becoming reality.

Dad said she had "lost her way," but I wasn't entirely convinced that she needed to change. Other than not going to church, the cursing and drinking, and the "stuff" she did with guys like Frank, she was perfect.

Okay, so maybe I was a little biased. There were worse crimes.

Why couldn't Madeline see that I really cared about her? She claimed that she didn't want me to complicate things, but she had also said that things were easier with me. She just didn't make any sense.

The more I thought about her, the madder I got. But I wasn't just mad at Madeline. I was mad at my parents and Jenn and Tony and even myself. I could feel the anger bubbling underneath my skin.

Feeling all that, I knew I should have stayed in my room until Mom left for church. But after hearing her call me four times—with me growing more and more annoyed each time—I went to the kitchen.

"Have a seat, honey," she said, a smile painted on her face. "Breakfast will be ready in a few minutes."

"I'm not hungry."

"Breakfast is the most important meal of the day." She wiped her perfectly clean hands on her perfectly white apron. "Now sit down."

I slinked to the table. Mom had already fixed a place setting for me, complete with matching silverware, a full glass of orange juice, and a steaming mug of coffee.

"Since when did you start fixing me coffee?"

She walked over to the table with a plate full of pancakes. "You seem to have a sudden appreciation for it. I figured I'd start serving it to you."

I stared at the mug. The coffee smelled strong enough to bring Lazarus back from the dead.

Mom put the plate of pancakes in front of me and sat down. "So your father talked to you about Madeline?"

I didn't know why she was asking. I was sure Dad had given her a play-by-play of our conversation.

"I know you're probably upset, but in time, you'll see that Madeline isn't the right type of girl for you."

"What do you know about Madeline?" I heard the spite in my voice, but I didn't care. "You said she couldn't be saved, right?"

Mom cleared her throat. "It's not that I think she can't find redemption. It's just . . . well, maybe once you're older, you'll understand."

"What's there to understand? You hate her."

Mom narrowed her eyes. "Joshua, I think I've had enough of that attitude." She shook her head. Then, under her breath but loud enough for me to hear, she said, "You were never like this when you dated Jennifer."

I pushed—or more like shoved—my plate away from me. "Jenn isn't the Little Miss Perfect you think she is," I said. "She was at the party the other night with her boyfriend." I paused, letting the tension build in the room. "Supposedly, they're having a lot of sex."

Mom's eyes flashed open. "Excuse me?"

"Sex, Mom." I shrugged, pretending to be nonchalant. "You know, when two people get naked and—"

"I know what sex is, Joshua." Mom's fingers twitched as she touched the edges of her hair, like she was making sure it was still there. "What I don't understand is why you feel the need to discuss it this morning."

"Look, you brought up Jenn, not me." I knew I should probably shut up, but I didn't want to. "From what I hear, they're really going at it, too. Like rabbits."

Mom immediately rose from the table. "I don't know what's gotten into you, but I don't like it. Your father should have never encouraged you to talk to Madeline."

I watched Mom scurry away to her room. I knew I should feel bad about the way I had spoken to her, but I was tired of her and Dad treating Madeline like a second-class citizen.

Madeline was a good person; she and everyone else in the world just seemed too stubborn to believe it.

* * *

The church service that morning dragged on forever. I sat in the choir stand, praying that Madeline would text me like she had last week.

Of course, my phone remained silent.

As soon as the service ended, I ran down the old dirt path to our hideaway, hoping she'd be there waiting to tell me how much she missed me, like our argument yesterday had never happened.

But when I reached our secret garden, I was greeted with humidity and silence.

Madeline hadn't changed her mind.

I didn't really feel like it, but I decided to drop by the nursing home after that. I didn't want to see the seniors, but I sure didn't want to go home, either. Upon entering the rec room, I found Leonard, Mr. Rollins, and Ms. Beatrice huddled in the corner. Leonard saw me and waved me over.

"What are y'all doing?" I asked.

"Eating," Leonard said between bites. "Jennifer stopped by and brought a few strawberry danishes."

"Not Jennifer," Ms. Beatrice said. "They're from Maddie."

I glanced around the room, like I had somehow overlooked her. "Madeline stopped by?"

"Yeah, and let me tell you, these danishes are a hell of a lot better than some old magazines." A glob of red jam hung at the corner of Mr. Rollins's mouth.

I took in a deep breath. I swore I could just make out the smell of vanilla and coffee.

"She left 'bout five minutes ago," Leonard said. "We told her you sometimes stop by after church, but that just made her move faster."

I rubbed the back of my neck. "We're not exactly on speaking terms right now."

"That's too bad," Ms. Beatrice said. "Y'all made such a cute couple. Y'all reminded me of me and my husband when we were courtin'."

Mr. Rollins took another bite of his danish. "You ain't missing out on nothin'. Like I said before, females ain't nothin' but trouble." He licked his finger. "Although I sho' do appreciate the sweets she brought by."

"You have diabetes," I said to Mr. Rollins. "You're not supposed to be eating things like that."

Mr. Rollins laughed. "At this point, diabetes is the last thing I'm worried 'bout." He coughed, and in doing so, dislodged the jam from his mouth. "The doctors say it won't be very long now. This lung has taken just about all it can."

Leonard shook his head. "Don't worry. Madeline

brought the low-sugar ones. And she made us promise we'd only give Rollins one of 'em."

Ms. Beatrice nodded toward an empty chair. "Have a seat, Joshua. You look like you could use some sweets."

I frowned and tried to remind myself that I was supposed to be mad at Madeline. "I'll pass."

"She left one for you," Leonard said. "She said if you showed up, we weren't to let you leave until you sat down and ate one with us."

I crossed my arms. "I don't like strawberries."

"She knows," Ms. Beatrice said. "That's why she left you a blackberry one."

chapter 14

After Dad found out about my little discussion with Mom, he grounded me for a week. I didn't even care.

The day after my punishment ended, Tony dropped by. "Josh, don't ever get into trouble like that again," he said as soon as I opened the door. He pushed past me and headed straight for my room. "You are seriously messing up my social life."

"And hello to you too," I said, following him down the hallway.

I wasn't sure if Tony even heard me. He had disappeared into my closet, his hands digging through my sweaters for his stash of condoms. While I wasn't a big fan of Tony and Charlotte's extracurricular activities, I was glad Tony was responsible enough to use protection. Unfortunately, he lived with two nosy parents and an even nosier sister. Thus, he got all the benefits of sex while I was saddled with keeping his condoms.

He emerged from the closet with two condoms in his hand and a dust bunny on his shoulder. "Thanks again, Josh. You know, you're welcome to dip into the stash as well."

"Um . . . I'll keep that in mind." I sat back on my bed, where my copy of *Invisible Man* lay waiting for me. Based on a suggestion from Madeline, I had checked out the book weeks ago but hadn't made it past the third chapter. "So what are you and Charlotte doing tonight?"

He grinned and looked at the condoms in his hand.

"I mean, before that." I fiddled with my fingernails, nervous as could be, even though I'd thought this through multiple times. "I was thinking maybe we could hang out tonight."

Tony grinned. "Wait a minute. I've been hounding you for months to go out, and now all of a sudden you're the one suggesting it?"

I shrugged. "I figured now was as good a time as any."

The smile faded from Tony's face as he plopped down beside me on the bed. "Sorry about the breakup with Madeline."

"It wasn't a breakup. We weren't even dating."

"Yeah, but still . . ."

"No, it's okay. Maybe it was the wake-up call I needed."
I glanced at Tony's compassionate face. So far, so good.
"So, what do you think? Can we all hang out tonight?"

Tony brushed the dust from his shirt. "Well, Charlotte
and I were planning to go to a movie, but I guess we can
make it a group thing."

"The movies? I was hoping we could do something more
social." I took a deep breath. "How about . . . bowling."

"Bowling? Are you kidding? No offense, but you're not
exactly the best bowler in the world."

"Yeah, I know, but I figured it'd be fun. Plus, it'd give
me a better opportunity to talk to girls."

Tony pressed his lips together. Finally, he nodded.
"Nothing good was showing at the movies anyway." He
rose from the bed. "Let me call Charlotte and see if she
can invite a few of her friends."

Tony and I walked back to the front door. "Thanks,
man. I really appreciate this."

"Hey, no problem." He opened the door. "I'm just surprised you want to go bowling. I thought you hated it."

I smiled. "I guess you could say I've had a change of
religion."

* * *

Tony was right, of course. I hated bowling, and I was
horrible at it. Every spring, the church had a "Bowling for
Jesus" tournament that raised money for the homeless.
My team always came in dead last.

As pathetic as it sounded, I was looking for any rea-
sonable excuse to bump into Madeline. Being that she

didn't return any of the messages I left for her, I knew I couldn't pop up at the coffee shop; that seemed too desperate. At least with bowling, I could maintain a small amount of self-respect.

I had called the bowling alley earlier that day. They limited league bowling to three days a week, including today, so I figured there was a pretty good chance that Frank would be there tonight.

Of course, Frank was the bowler, not Madeline, so even if he was there tonight, there was no guarantee that she'd be with him. She could have easily been working, or hanging out at home, or perhaps she and Frank could have skipped the bowling alley altogether in order to do God-knows-what. But just the possibility of her being there was enough motivation to go.

Upon entering, I scanned the lanes but didn't see her. Before I could look any further, I spotted Tony and Charlotte waving me over to a table.

Charlotte stood and hugged me while Tony stuffed the last bit of a corn dog into his mouth. Then he mumbled something, but I couldn't understand a word.

"He says hello," Charlotte translated.

"How could you possibly understand what he just said?"

"It's a gift." She shrugged. "He actually said you should quit slowpoking and get your shoes, but I was trying to give you the abridged version." She nodded toward a lane. "I called up a few of my friends, and they've already reserved a lane."

I looked at Charlotte's friends, all cool-looking, with their designer jeans and perfect hair. They reminded me of the kind of people at her party—the kind that usually didn't want anything to do with me.

"Now hurry up and get your shoes," Charlotte said. "Rachel's already in line."

My heart sank. *Rachel.* I had hoped that Tony and Charlotte hadn't invited her, but I should have known better.

Rachel waved at me as I neared the counter. She was decked out in makeup and a top that showed off a little too much of her stomach. I wondered if it was for my benefit.

"I didn't know you were coming out tonight," I said.

She smiled. She had gotten a lot better at applying lip gloss. "Charlotte's trying to hook me up with one of her friends."

I looked back at the lane. "The one with the earrings or the one wearing the sunglasses?" I knew neither of those guys were the object of her affection, but I had to ask.

She shook her head. "Good Lord, no. Those guys are more into hair care than I am."

"Good. They're probably too old for you, anyway."

"Why do you say that?" She twirled a strand of hair around her pointy index finger. "Seniors can be as immature as sophomores."

"What would your parents say if they knew you were trying to date someone two years older?"

Rachel started doing that whole giggling thing again. "Well, that all depends on the guy."

I took a step forward, away from Rachel. The line wasn't moving nearly fast enough.

All of a sudden, Rachel stopped laughing. "So what happened between you and that girl you were seeing?" She placed her hand on my arm. "Why'd y'all break up?"

I stared at her hand. Her fingers were bony. Light. Nothing like Madeline's.

"Well . . ." I thought about trying to explain the technicalities of ending a nonrelationship, but instead I shook my head. "I'm not really sure why things ended like they did."

Rachel nodded toward the door. "Well, just so you're not surprised, she's here. With another guy."

I spun around. Sure enough, Madeline and a guy I assumed to be Frank stood just inside the entrance. Madeline wore a pair of black boots and a denim skirt. Her blouse was tight and low-cut.

Frank carried a small bowling bag. With his free hand, he waved to a bunch of people on the other side of the building. Then he leaned extremely close to Madeline, whispered something into her ear, and headed off. She started toward the counter, but stopped as soon as our gazes met.

Madeline looked stunned. At first, I thought she was going to run off in the opposite direction. But after a few seconds of hovering, she headed toward me. She could only take mini-steps, her skirt was so tight.

"I'd better go talk to her," I said to Rachel.

"But what about your shoes?"

I heard her, but I couldn't have responded if I'd wanted to. My brain was too busy trying to formulate what I was going to say to Madeline.

I met her halfway between the entrance and the counter. "Hey."

"Hey, Joshua." She glanced behind me. "Who's that? Your new girlfriend?"

I looked back at Rachel as she stared Madeline down. "That's Tony's little sister."

"She's cute."

"She's fifteen."

"Two years isn't that much of an age difference," Madeline said. "Frank is four years older than me."

I looked toward the other side of the bowling alley, where Madeline's *man* was talking with a group of guys. "I heard you went by the nursing home," I said. "That was nice of you."

"I like the old-timers. They don't bullshit you. They tell you exactly what's on their mind." She laughed. "Plus, I think Mr. Rollins has a crush on me."

Talking to her now, listening to her laugh, breathing in her smell, it was almost like that talk at her house had never happened. How could people who got along so well just up and decide to stop talking to each other?

"They really liked the danishes," I said. "Thanks for leaving one for me as well."

Madeline looked down as she tucked a strand of hair behind her ear. "They were just some old pastries we were going to throw out anyway. I figured I'd give them to folks who would appreciate them."

From the corner of my eye, I could see that Tony and Charlotte had already started the game. Madeline must have noticed too. "You'd better go. You shouldn't keep your friends waiting."

I stepped in her path, blocking her from escaping. "Maybe I can come by the coffee shop sometime."

"Joshua . . ."

"I miss talking to you." I took another step toward her and placed my hand on her hip. She didn't move closer to me, but she didn't back away, either. "Don't you miss talking to me?"

"Yes, but . . . it's complicated." She placed her hand on mine. "You wouldn't understand."

"Try me. Just tell me—"

"What's taking you so long? I thought you'd have that pitcher by now."

Both Madeline and I jumped. I turned to see Frank grimacing at me.

"Sorry, baby." Madeline dropped her hand and backed away from me. "This is my friend Joshua. The one I told you about."

Frank's face immediately relaxed. He even smiled. "Yeah, the preacher's kid." He shook my hand. "I've heard a lot of good things about you."

Unfortunately, I could not say the same about him.

Frank wrapped his arm around Madeline's waist; his hand settled right where mine had just rested. "Now, I know y'all are friends and all, but don't go turning Madeline into some type of saint."

"Me, a saint?" She wrapped her arms around his neck.

165

"You know me, baby. Why be good when it's funner to be bad?"

Funner? Madeline was too smart to sound so stupid.

"The guys are about to start the next game." Frank patted Madeline's butt, and I swear to God, I wanted to punch him. "I'm going to grab that pitcher."

"I'll meet you at the lane, baby." Her voice was as sweet and artificial as cherry-flavored bubble gum.

"Joshua, nice to meet you," Frank said, before heading toward the counter.

"Nice guy," I mumbled once he was out of range.

"He'll do, for now."

All I could do was frown.

Madeline crossed her arms. "I'm sorry you don't like what you see, but this is who I am now. A girl who just likes to have fun. Nothing more, nothing less."

"You know this isn't you." And before she could respond, I turned and marched toward the exit.

It wasn't until I reached the door that I realized that, for once, I was glad to leave.

*   *   *

Bzzzz. Bzzzz.

I reached over and slapped the top of my alarm clock.

Bzzzz. Bzzzz.

I cracked my eyelids open and let my vision adjust to the dark. The alarm clock read 3:24.

I sat up and followed the buzzing sound to the other side of the room. My cell phone was jumping across the top of my desk like it was dancing.

166

I grabbed the phone and looked at the screen. Madeline.

"Hello?" I said, my voice full of sleep and fear.

"Meet me outside. Now." The line went dead.

Is she serious? Does she really expect me to—

Suddenly, a car horn blared from outside my window.

Yep. She's serious.

I grabbed my robe, stuffed my feet into my sneakers, and crept out of my room. Luckily, it was on the first floor, adjacent to the kitchen. I only hoped Madeline's honking hadn't woken up my parents.

I paused at the base of the stairs, straining my ears for the slightest hint of sound. But after standing in silence for a few minutes, I headed to the kitchen and slipped outside.

Madeline leaned against her aunt's car. As soon as she saw me, she marched my way.

"Madeline, what's going on?" I whispered. "Do you know what time it is? Is everything all right?"

As Madeline got closer, I saw streaks of mascara on her cheeks. She still wore her black boots and jean skirt, but she moved a lot quicker now than she had earlier that night.

She planted her hands on her hips. "You are such a bastard."

"What?"

"You know how I feel about my dad. And you *still* called him!"

"Madeline, calm down." I pulled her farther away from the house. "What are you talking about?"

"You know damn well what I'm talking about!" She

poked me in the chest so hard that I almost fell over. "You called Dad and told him I was a slut. And now he's forcing Aunt Gwen to kick me out of the house!"

"Of course I didn't—"

My head jerked to the side as her hand exploded against my cheek. *"Don't you dare fucking lie to me!"*

Heat and pain radiated across my face. "Madeline, I don't even know what you're talking about!" As my eyes regained their focus, I saw a porch light switch on across the street.

Madeline reached back to slap me again, but this time, I grabbed her hands and pinned them to her sides. "Will you please calm down and tell me what's going on?"

Tears streamed down her face. "All I know is that my dad is coming this weekend to take me back to Virginia." She sniffled. "He said I was morally corrupt. He said he was coming to stop me from ruining someone else's life."

"I promise, I didn't call him." I kept a tight grip on her arms. "But maybe he should come down and talk to you—"

"No! I hate him!" She twisted enough to get one arm free, but I quickly grabbed it and pinned it back in place. "I don't want anything to do with him!"

Behind me, the back door swung open and our porch light flickered on. I glanced over my shoulder and watched Dad shuffle onto the steps. "Joshua, what's going on out here?"

"Nothing, Dad. Madeline and I were just talking."

"No, it's not *nothing*." She continued to struggle to get out of my grip. "All you preachers are alike. You think you can control everybody."

Dad strode over to us. "Young lady, you need to bring your voice down."

"And you need to stay out of other people's business!" She turned to me and finally stopped wrangling in my grip. "You've got five seconds to get your goddamn hands off me."

"Do you promise to calm down?"

"I promise that if you don't let me go, your dad will have to pry my hands away from your throat."

Well, at least she was speaking calmly now. I slowly released her.

She rubbed her wrists. "And I thought you really cared about me."

"I do care about—"

"Fuck you, Joshua Wynn." She flipped me the finger. "Fuck both of y'all. I'm out of here."

"Madeline, wait!" I ran after her, but I might as well have been yelling at a brick wall. Madeline stormed to her car, refusing to even look in my direction. A few seconds later, she roared down the street.

I watched the smoke from the car's exhaust dissipate into the darkness. "I just don't understand. . . ."

"Let's talk more inside," Dad said. "We've already woken up enough of the neighborhood tonight."

I followed Dad into the kitchen, where Mom was already waiting. "Will someone please explain what's going on? I was about to call the police."

I sunk into a chair. "Madeline is mad. Really mad. And I don't have any idea why." I rubbed my face; no doubt my cheek was red from that slap. "She thinks I called her father and said horrible things about her." I turned to Dad. "You didn't call him, did you?"

"I haven't talked to him since the day after Charlotte's party," he said.

I shook my head; my face started to sting even more. *Why in the world would she think I called her dad? What would give her that—*

I snapped my head up and looked at Mom. Her gaze was glued to the floor.

"It was you, wasn't it?"

Mom nodded, her mouth grim. "Yes, I called Greg."

Dad scratched his head. "Why didn't you say anything to me about this?"

"I've been saying something ever since Madeline showed back up." Mom clutched her silk robe shut in one hand, bracing herself against the wall with the other. "I'm sorry, Joshua, but Madeline is capsizing! I couldn't stand around and let her pull you down right along with her."

"She's not—"

"She sleeps around. She drinks and does drugs, and Lord knows what else." Mom tightened her grip on her robe. "I wanted to see the good in her, I really did, but I can't take that chance anymore. You've just been so disrespectful lately. And then when I found those condoms in your room—"

"You went through my stuff?" I jumped from my seat. "You searched my room?"

Her gaze dropped to the floor again. "I found them by accident."

I snorted. There was no way Mom could have "accidentally" stumbled across those condoms.

"You know, I don't even care that you went through my stuff. Just tell me—did you call Madeline a slut?"

Dad stepped beside me. "Joshua, why don't you calm down—"

"Did you call her a slut or not, Mom?"

"Of course not. You know I'd never use that type of language. All I did was tell Greg the truth—that his daughter was morally irresponsible and was a danger to my child."

I squeezed my hands into fists. "Thanks to you, her aunt is being forced to kick her out of the house. Now she doesn't have anywhere to go but back to her parents' house."

"Are you sure?" Dad asked. "I know Greg's strict, but surely he's not that strict."

"Your father's right—there must be some mistake." Mom cleared her throat. "While I did strongly suggest that he come down here and deal with Madeline, I never asked him to kick her out."

I turned my gaze to our tiled kitchen floor. I was afraid what would happen if I continued looking at my parents. "I'm not making a mistake about this. Her father is coming down here to drag Madeline back to Virginia, whether she wants to go or not."

"Well, perhaps it's for the best that she goes back home," Mom said. "They can give her the support she needs."

Mom obviously knew nothing about what was best for Madeline. But I shouldn't have been surprised—she didn't even know what was best for me anymore.

I watched their shadows, long and oblique, as they moved toward me. I backed away.

"Joshua, please. Say something," Mom said. "I know you're upset, but maybe—"

"You know what?" I let out a deep, sarcastic laugh. "This is really fucked up."

Mom and Dad inhaled sharply. For a second, all time stopped.

"Joshua, you need to watch your language," Dad finally said.

I hated that my eyes were watering. "We're supposed to help people. How is this going to help Madeline?"

"Madeline has some serious demons," Dad said. "If anyone can help her, her family—"

"This is wrong." I pointed to Mom. "*She's* wrong."

Dad narrowed his eyes. "She's my wife, and she's your mother. You *will* show her some respect."

I tried to back up more, but I had already been forced against the wall.

"This isn't just about Madeline," he said. "We're trying to look out for your best interests as well." Dad placed a hand on my shoulder. "You're young. You're highly impressionable."

I shook his hand off me. "This is fucked up!"

Dad held his hands up and backed away. "I think you'd better go to bed before you say something else you'll regret."

"I don't regret anything I've said tonight." I cut my eyes toward my mother. "I'm not the one who did something wrong."

chapter 15

Three days later, I still hadn't spoken to Mom. I was actually glad the youth group was heading to Savannah for our retreat. It would be a lot easier to avoid Mom if we weren't sleeping under the same roof.

I hadn't talked to Madeline either, but not for lack of trying. That morning, like every other morning, I had tried to call her cell. Usually, I got sent directly to voice mail, but today, I got a message saying her service had been disconnected.

I stepped onto the bus hoping to find an empty seat, but most were occupied by at least one other person. Rachel spotted me, timidly smiled, and moved over a little in her seat. I didn't really want to sit beside her—I didn't think I could stand sitting through three hours of giggling—but the only other available seats were across from Donna and Dora, and I sure didn't want to sit next to them.

I plopped down beside Rachel. "You couldn't convince Tony to come?"

"Are you kidding? He and Charlotte are practically joined at the hip. Ever since they . . . well, *you know* . . . it's like they can't go ten minutes without talking to each other."

"So you know about Tony and Charlotte?"

She nodded. "You should see the way they look at each other. It's like they can't wait to—"

"Please. No details." I squinted at Rachel and focused on her eyes. "Hey—what happened to all the makeup?"

Rachel brought her hand to her face. "Do you know how long it takes to put that stuff on every day? I like makeup, but not more than those twenty minutes of sleep I gain back by not putting it on." She looked down at her lap. "It didn't seem to be doing much good, anyway."

Maybe it was the softness of her voice, but for some reason, I wanted to comfort her. I took her chin and tilted her face up. It was funny—her lips were shaped similarly to Madeline's. "You look better without the makeup."

Rachel smiled, and I momentarily forgot that she was my best friend's fifteen-year-old sister.

Suddenly aware of how I was holding her face, I let go of her chin. "Um . . . I'd better go see what the holdup is."

I scampered down the aisle. Rachel was way too young

for me. Plus, as much as I wished otherwise, she wasn't Madeline.

As I stepped off the bus, I pulled my phone out and stared at the blank screen. Before I lost my nerve, I punched in her aunt's phone number.

"Hello? Madeline?" her aunt answered.

"No, this is Joshua."

"Oh. Hello, Joshua. I'm sorry. I was praying this was Madeline." Her voice sounded dry and scratchy. "By any chance, have you seen her lately?"

"Not since she showed up at my house a few days ago." I glanced behind me, where the driver was loading the last of the suitcases. "Is something wrong?"

"The last time I saw her was when she said she was going to talk to you, three days ago. I just assumed she was trying to blow off some steam, but by the time I woke up the next morning, she was gone." Ms. Smith sniffled on the other end of the phone. "I knew she was upset about her father forcing her to move back home, but I never expected her to run off."

I moved farther away from the bus. "What about her clothes?"

"All gone. All she left was my car keys on the table," she said. "She called me two days ago and said she was okay and staying with a friend. She wouldn't tell me anything else."

"Do you think she's staying with Frank?"

"I have no idea. I don't even know enough about the boy to look up his address in the phone book." I could tell

Ms. Smith was crying now. "If she only came back home, I'd find a way for her to stay with me, even if Greg kicked us both out," she said. "I don't even like the damn house that much."

I looked around. I was the only person not on the bus.

"Maybe I could find her." From the corner of my eye, I watched as Mrs. Anderson waddled down the bus steps. "That is, if she hasn't left town yet."

"No, I don't want to pull you from whatever you're doing. I just need to sit tight and—"

"Please, let me help." Even though it was Mom, not me, who had helped get Madeline into this mess, I still felt guilty. Maybe this was God's way of giving me a second chance.

She sighed. "Well, it *would* make me feel a little better. . . ."

"Then it's settled," I said. "I'll find her, and I'll bring her back home. I promise."

I flipped my phone shut just as Mrs. Anderson reached me. "Let's go, Joshua." She tapped her clipboard. "We're going to be late if we don't leave now."

I looked at the itinerary in Mrs. Anderson's thick fingers. "I don't think I'm going to be able to make the trip."

"And why not?"

I leaned back as she glared at me. "It's kind of hard to explain."

"Joshua, you're the president of the youth group. What would your father say—"

"I'm sorry, Mrs. Anderson, but the youth group can

take care of itself." I backed away from her. "Maybe I can drive to Savannah tomorrow morning."

She shook her head. "If you're not on this bus when we pull out of the parking lot, don't bother making the trip."

I glanced at the bus. Rachel pressed her face against the window, her eyes filled with worry. I flashed her a half smile before turning back to Mrs. Anderson. "I'm sorry, but I can't go."

I waved good-bye to Rachel's frowning face, then headed to my car, not even bothering to grab my suitcase from the bus. As I slid behind the steering wheel, I focused on my father's white Cadillac parked in front of the sanctuary. I knew I should run into the church and explain to him why I was skipping the trip, but after a few seconds, I decided against it. I was looking for Madeline, and like she had said before, girls like her didn't go to church.

*   *   *

I spent all afternoon cruising the city. I went to all the usual places where I thought Madeline could be—the coffee shop, the community college campus, the bowling alley, and even the nursing home. My phone lit up with calls from my parents, Tony, and Rachel. I ignored them all.

On my fifth trip to the bowling alley, I spotted Frank—sans Madeline—at the far end of the building.

I wiped my sweaty hands on my jeans as I marched toward his lane. Frank frowned as I got closer, but not like he was mad at me. It was more like he couldn't quite place me. A cigarette dangled at the corner of his mouth, and smoke billowed from his nose.

I stuck out my hand. "Joshua Wynn."

His eyes brightened. "Madeline's friend, right?" He shook my hand. "How's the hellion doing?" I was amazed he could talk without removing the cigarette from his lips.

"That's why I'm here." I stood up straight and tall, as if that would make me more imposing. "Her aunt hasn't seen her in a few days. I hoped you might know where she is."

"Sorry, but I haven't seen her either." He removed the cigarette from his mouth to take a sip of beer. "She dumped me, although I ain't really broken up about it. I kind of lost interest in her." He winked. "She hadn't been putting out like she used to. I guess she didn't have enough free milk to pass around."

I crossed my arms. "I wouldn't know."

Frank took a long drag of the cigarette before propping it on the corner of an ashtray. "You got to be shittin' me. All that time y'all spent together, I just figured she had moved on to you."

"You figured wrong." What did Madeline ever see in this guy?

"Well, it's your loss." Frank picked up his bowling ball and wiped it off with a cloth. "Hold on a sec." He ambled to the lane, repositioned the ball in his hands, and then hurled it down toward the pins.

They exploded in every direction.

He walked back to me, pausing to high-five the other bowlers. "Like I said before, I haven't seen her." He picked up his cigarette and knocked a few loose ashes from the end. "If you ever find her, do me a favor and get my shirt back."

* * *

Four hours and umpteen prayers later, I stood at the entrance of the reggae club. The same bouncer who had allowed me in before stood at the door. He looked even larger than last time.

I cautiously smiled at him. "I don't know if you remember me, but—"

"Of course I know who you are. You're Pastor Wynn's kid."

I frowned. "If you knew who I was, why'd you let me into the club that night?"

He cracked a smile. "Madeline's a friend. She said that if I let you in, she'd keep you out of trouble." He stepped back and let a couple of guys exit the building. "She seemed really sad when she showed up tonight."

I lunged forward. "Is she still here?" I asked, my voice cracking. "I really need to see her. It's important."

He stared at me long and hard, and then moved out of the way. "You know the rules. No smoking. No drinking." He picked up a rubber stamp and motioned for my hand. This time, I remembered to offer it palm-down.

I went into the building, paid the cashier, and slid into the club. It took a second for my eyes to adjust to the darkness and smoke. I knew she would be either on the dance floor or at the bar.

The dance floor was just about empty. I moved my gaze

to the bar, and immediately spotted her. As always, she looked sexy. And dangerous. Her red halter top dipped low on her chest, and her black shorts could have been mistaken for underwear, they were so short.

I strode to the bar and pulled up a stool beside her. She didn't look surprised to see me. She might have even smirked.

"Aunt Gwen send you?"

I nodded. "She's worried about you."

Madeline grabbed her purse and pulled out a pack of cigarettes. She leaned over to the guy next to her. "Got a light?"

He whipped out a Bic and lit her cigarette. She puffed on it a few seconds; the end changed from white to red to dark gray. She leaned her head back, blew smoke into the air, and then flicked a few ashes into an already full ashtray.

Smoking is the only thing I don't do, I remembered Madeline telling me. But I didn't say anything. I just watched her take puff after puff. The cigarette slowly burned itself away.

"I have so many other bad habits, I figured one more couldn't hurt." Smoke escaped from her mouth as she talked. "You want to try to convince me to stop smoking?"

"I learned a long time ago that I can't force you to do anything you don't want to do." I gestured toward the bottles of alcohol. "No tequila tonight?"

"Chris won't serve me any more. Says I've had my limit." She glared at him. "Jackass."

I moved closer to her. I couldn't smell her usual coffee-and-vanilla scent under all the smoke and alcohol. "Maybe you should go home."

"I don't have a home to go to."

"Your aunt says you can come back and stay with her. She's not kicking you out, no matter what your dad does. She said she'd even move."

"Even if she wanted to, Aunt Gwen can't afford to move anywhere else. Plus, I've already gotten her into enough trouble." She ground what little remained of the cigarette into the ashtray. "I get everyone into trouble."

Madeline fished another cigarette from her purse and propositioned the guy next to her for another light. As she took a puff, she stared at my cheek.

"If I said I was sorry for slapping you, would you believe me?"

I nodded.

"Just so we're clear, I'm apologizing for hitting you. I'm not sorry for what I said."

"But I didn't do anything."

"It's guilt by association. If your parents were to blame, they only did it because you wouldn't leave me alone."

"You know, I haven't spoken to my mom since that night," I said. "I cursed at her."

Madeline arched an eyebrow. "Really? What did you say?"

"I dropped the f bomb. Twice."

"Man, you must have been really upset."

"I was." I locked my eyes with hers. "I really do care about you."

Her gaze melted a little. "I know. And that's why you shouldn't . . . why I can't . . ." She shook her head. "God, I need a drink. This is not a time to be sober."

"Where have you been staying?"

"At some trashy motel." She blew a smoke ring from her mouth. "I can pick up my check from the coffee shop tomorrow. As soon as I cash it, I'm out."

"But what about school?"

"Community college isn't exactly Harvard. I can always start again." She finished her second cigarette. "Tell Aunt Gwen I'll call her as soon as I get to wherever I'm going."

My heartbeat intensified as she slipped off her stool. "Are you leaving?"

"There's no point in sticking around if the bartender won't serve me. I think I have a bottle of tequila at the motel."

"Don't go." I jumped from my seat. "You want to dance?"

"I can't dance when I'm not happy," she said as she walked off.

I rushed after her. "But you've been drinking. You can't drive."

"Of course I can't drive. I don't have a car," she said. "I'll call a cab."

"But—"

"Thanks for checking up on me, sweetie, but this isn't

your element." Madeline patted my cheek. "You need to go home. You don't belong here."

"Why don't you come home with me? I'm sure if we talk—"

"I'm through with talking," she said. "I'm going back to my room, finding that bottle of tequila, and getting drunk. And unless you plan on drinking, you're not invited."

I grabbed her hand. "Fine. Let's get drunk."

chapter 16

The Palmetto Paradise Motel looked nothing like its namesake—unless paradise was filled with broken plastic flamingos, browning palm trees, and rusted, overflowing Dumpsters. A huge, grime-covered neon sign blinked on and off as we pulled up.

"Which room?" I asked.

"The one with the peeling green paint on the door."

I rolled my eyes. "Thanks. That narrows it down considerably."

"Room one-twenty-two. It's in the back."

I rounded the building and parked in front of her room. As Madeline stepped out of the car, she tripped.

"Fucking heels." She leaned over and slipped out of her shoes. "I hate these things. I feel like a giant every time I stand up."

"If you hate them, why do you wear them?"

"Because that's what girls are supposed to do."

I stared at her feet as she rummaged through her purse. The concrete sidewalk looked like pigeons had been deliberately aiming at it for weeks. "Do you think it's a good idea to be walking around without shoes on?"

"Believe me, the carpet isn't much better." She pulled her keys from her purse and unlocked the door. "It ain't much, but at least my father can't kick me out of it."

I followed Madeline into the room. A pile of clothes was heaped in the middle of the queen-size bed. Her other clothes were bursting from the two suitcases on the floor. An empty pizza box sat on a small desk, with a column of books stacked on the accompanying chair.

"Have a seat, if you can find the room. And don't worry, all the clothes on the bed are clean."

I sat on the corner of the bed while Madeline rummaged around in the pile, her hands tossing an assortment of bras and underwear to the side. When one of her haphazardly thrown bras grazed my knee, I almost fell off the bed.

I tugged at my collar, trying to cool my scorching skin. I had no idea what I was getting myself into, but I wasn't about to up and bail out now. I hadn't come this far just to fail.

She finally pulled a half-full bottle of alcohol from her

pile. "I knew it was in here." She tapped her fingernails against the glass. "This is one of the only good things I got from Frank."

"He says hello, by the way. And he wants his shirt back."

Madeline sat beside me and unscrewed the cap. "You really were looking all over the place for me, weren't you?"

"Like I said, we were worried."

She tipped her head back and took a long swallow from the bottle. Her face twisted in its usual way. "All my glasses are dirty," she mumbled after she had swallowed.

I took the bottle from her. The gold liquid sloshed around like it was trying to forge an escape.

Madeline placed her hand on my thigh, causing my entire body to twitch. "Joshua, you don't really have to do it if you don't want to."

At that point, I had already tipped up the bottle. I collected a bit of tequila into my cheeks. I wanted to swallow it, but my throat wasn't cooperating.

"You look like a chipmunk," she said as she took the bottle from me. "You're supposed to drink it, not store it for the winter."

I took a deep breath and swallowed. All the way down, the tequila set my throat ablaze. I exploded into a coughing fit.

"Are you okay?" She slapped me on the back.

My eyes were like lawn sprinklers. "Lungs. On. Fire," I wheezed, before being overtaken by another bout of coughing.

"Don't take such a big sip next time," she said.

After a few moments, I was finally able to sit up. I wiped my eyes. "What is that stuff?"

"Jose Cuervo. The good shit." She screwed the cap back on. "Maybe you shouldn't be drinking with me."

"I always keep my word." I took the bottle back from her. "Even when it involves drinking gasoline."

"Well, give it a second before you drink again. The last thing I want you doing is coughing up my good liquor." Madeline reached over me to her pile of clothes. "Close your eyes."

"Why?" I asked, although I was already doing as she requested.

"I want to get out of this top, and I don't want you staring at my precious cargo while I change."

A surge of energy flashed through me as I heard the rustling of clothes. "Why don't you just go to the bathroom?"

"I'm lazy. And it'll only take a second." She tapped me on the arm. "You can open your eyes now."

I opened them, and my gaze immediately shot to her chest. Her not-quite-thick-enough T-shirt used to have lettering on it, but it looked to have faded away long ago. She also wasn't wearing a bra.

"Stop staring," she said.

I looked back up. "Sorry."

She laughed, but not really in a happy kind of way. "Don't feel bad. Everyone stares." She leaned against the headboard and closed her eyes. "You can probably try another sip now."

I unscrewed the cap and brought the purple-lined rim to my mouth. Then I almost hacked up a lung.

Madeline remained motionless as I struggled for breath. "So what part of this is supposed to be fun?" I asked.

"Just relax," she said. "You can't rush the feeling. It takes a few minutes for the alcohol to take effect."

I placed the bottle on the floor and picked up one of the books lodged underneath the pile of clothes. All throughout the book, pieces of text were highlighted in yellow and purple. In the margins, notes were scribbled in purple ink.

"Purple." I flipped the book shut. "It's the color of royalty, you know."

Her eyes still closed, she nodded. "It's also the color of lesbianism." She smirked. "And no, I'm not a lesbian."

We remained silent for a few moments—Madeline with her eyes closed, and me staring at the darkness of her lips and the shape of her body.

"Did you ever read *The Color Purple*?" she asked.

"No, but I saw the movie once."

"Anyone I've ever talked to who's read the book always wants to talk about Celie. How bad she was treated. How mean everyone was to her." Madeline's eyes fluttered open. "Most folks are so focused on Celie, they forget about Shug." She shook her head. "People always forget about Shug."

I wished I had paid more attention to the movie. It had been years since I had seen it, and even then, I didn't really like it that much. It was too depressing.

She sat up and picked up the bottle. "You having fun yet?"

"Of course. Can't you tell from my labored breathing and the look of pain on my face?"

She motioned for me to move closer. "I know a good drinking game we can play. It's like truth or dare, just without the dares."

"I've never played truth or dare. It's not the type of game you play on church retreats."

She rolled her eyes. "The game is called shot of truth. If someone takes a shot of tequila, the other person has to say something truthful. And it has to be profound, not some shit like 'My socks are green.'"

I yanked my pant legs up and pointed to my plain white tube socks. "My socks aren't green."

"No, they aren't." She took a sip of tequila. "Start talking."

I rubbed my face and thought for a few seconds. "This is kind of tough. My life must not be very profound."

She sighed and pushed the bottle toward me. "Maybe I should go first. Drink up."

Much more slowly, I tilted my head back and took a swig of tequila. It still burned.

"Okay, I hate my father–"

"That's not profound!" My voice sounded like I was talking in slow motion.

"You interrupted me before I could finish." She thumped me on the arm. "As I was saying, I hate my father, but he isn't really my dad. I'm adopted."

189

"Really? How long have you known?"

"I just found out a few years ago. When we were arguing, he blurted out something about the fruit not falling far from the tree. I didn't think Mom had ever been 'deceitful and scandalous,' so I pressed the issue. He eventually broke down and told me the truth."

I fanned at the sweat collecting behind my ears. "Do you want to meet her? Your real mom?"

"Maybe, but my folks won't give me any information about her. They just said she was really messed up and that I was lucky to have ended up with them."

"What about your sisters? Are they adopted?"

"Nope, they're lucky enough to have been sired by the old man himself. As soon as Deborah was born, I could tell things were going to be different between me and Dad. It didn't get any better when Hannah was born two years later." She took the bottle, but didn't immediately drink. "I really miss them. Especially Hannah. Dad wouldn't even let me come home once I got kicked out of Trinity. Made me stay in a Motel Six on the other side of town until he could ship me down here."

"Then maybe that's a good reason to go home. You'd have a chance to see your sisters."

"Believe me, Dad doesn't want me home. He might have said he was coming to pick me up, but I promise, there is no way he's ever letting me back into that house." Madeline wiped her eyes with the back of her hand, then drank. "Okay, I've talked enough. Your turn."

"But—"

"Your turn," she repeated. "Get to it."

I thought for a few moments. Madeline just stared at me, not saying anything, which made me more nervous.

Finally, I sighed. "I'm a virgin, and I'm not sure why."

Madeline bit her bottom lip while grinning at me. "Technically, you're a virgin because you haven't had sex yet."

"I'm a virgin because I'm supposed to be a virgin. I'm good because I'm supposed to be good. I do whatever my parents say, without even thinking about whether it's what I want to do. It's like I don't have an original opinion in my body. I'm full of shit, and no one seems to care."

"What about basketball? That's original, right? I didn't think your dad liked sports."

"He just likes golf. But *the church* thought it would be a good idea to form a team, so I played. And I really loved it. I wish I could try out for the school basketball team. But I can't, because I'm too busy organizing youth revivals and visiting nursing homes, and doing all the other shit that I think will make him proud."

"Well, I'm sure he wouldn't be proud to hear you say *shit* so much. And don't talk bad about the old-timers. They're really cool."

"I know, but come on. I am the most pathetic seventeen-year-old in the history of seventeen-year-olds. I didn't even start cursing until three days ago."

"At least you're not a slut," Madeline said. "It's much safer to be a good kid than a slut. And it's easier on the knees."

I winced. "I really hate it when you say stuff like that." I leaned back into her pile of clothes; it took too much energy to sit upright. "You're really smart, and really pretty. You don't have to act so slutty."

She didn't say anything for a few moments, before finally leaning over and handing me the bottle. "Drink first. Then I'll talk."

I drank and nestled the bottle in my arms. The fire in my throat had calmed to an almost warm sensation.

"I lost my virginity when I was fifteen, but I didn't lose it to my boyfriend, Carlos. The guy's name was Thomas. Everyone else called him Pastor Grant."

I pushed myself back up. "You slept with a preacher?"

"He was just out of seminary, and had come on board to help guide our youth group. He was supposed to be helping me form the praise-dance team."

"Wow. An actual preacher."

"It gets worse. He was married. His wife was a schoolteacher." She looked up at the water-stained ceiling. "I was a pro at home-wrecking before I could even drive."

I placed my hand on her leg and slipped my fingers underneath her calf. Surprisingly, her legs hadn't changed much from when she was a child. She had always had strong legs. Dancer's legs. Runner's legs.

"Madeline, you realize you were taken advantage of, right? You were raped."

"It wasn't rape."

"You were a minor. He wasn't. That's statutory rape."

"I loved him. I knew exactly what I was doing." She

crossed her arms. "And I'm through talking about it. That swig only buys so much truth."

"Fine." I swallowed another gulp of Madeline's truth serum. "Did your dad ever find out about it?"

Madeline stared at me with red eyes. "If it was up to me, I would have never told my dad," she said. "It was Thomas. In one of his many periods of weakness, he told him."

"What did your dad do to him?"

"He forgave him—said that I must have tempted him." Much to my surprise, her voice was even. Steady. Unflinching. "Later that night, Dad confronted me. He said I was damaged goods. That I was a temptress and a whore." She pressed her foot against my thigh. "The only good that came out of it was that my doctor finally put me on the pill."

I didn't know if it was the tequila or Madeline's revelation that was making it so hard for me to concentrate. "Wait. Your father blamed *you*?"

"Don't be surprised. If most of Christianity can blame Eve for getting Adam kicked out of the Garden of Eden, surely my father can blame me for tempting a preacher." She took the bottle. "And like I said before, I knew what I was doing. It was my fault."

"But the preacher—"

"Enough with the questions," she said. "Why don't you call your parents? They're probably worried."

I pulled my cell phone from my pocket and turned it on. I wanted to dial the number, but all the buttons bled together.

I dropped my phone into her mass of clothes. "I'm hammered."

"You're not even tipsy." She drank. "Give it a few more swigs. Then you'll be good and trashed."

I collapsed backward on the bed. I wanted to think about something profound in my life, some big secret to reveal, but I was drowning in an information overload.

"Hey, are you falling asleep?" She nudged me with her toe. "You owe me a truth."

"I'm just thinking. About you."

"Really?" The mattress shook, and a few seconds later, Madeline appeared. She straddled my hips. "What exactly are you thinking about me?"

I glanced at her chest. "Due in part to your provocative attire, I've been thinking a lot of things. But right now, all I can think about is you and the preacher."

Her face fell. "Like I said, I'm a slut."

I squinted at her, trying to focus. "Whether you want to admit it or not, you were taken advantage of. Your dad made you believe it was your fault, and once you fell for what he was saying, it was easy to let him and your family and your boyfriends and everyone else treat you like shit."

"That's enough, Joshua."

"You got scared, so you did what was easy. You acted like a slut, and you slept around, and you experimented. It validated what you did with the preacher."

Madeline returned to the far end of the bed. "I think you've had enough to drink for tonight."

Even though the room was starting to spin, I crawled to her. "I'm not finished." I took her face in my hands and turned it so that her eyes locked with mine. "You drank, so now you get to hear the truth whether you like it or not."

"I promise, if you don't shut up, I'm going to slap you again." Her voice, which had just sounded so strong and secure, now cracked. "I don't want to talk about this any-more!"

My head was beginning to throb, but I refused to stop. "You're a fake. You're not the slut everyone thinks you are. You're not the type of girl who jumps from bed to bed." I moved even closer to her. "You're the kind of girl who brings pastries to old people and kisses seventeen-year-old virgins. You're a good person."

Madeline blinked a few times as a tear rolled down her cheek. I let go of her face. "You can slap me now if you still want to."

And apparently she still wanted to, because Madeline sure did slap me. But before the air had even hit my bruised skin, she grabbed me and sucked me into a kiss.

The tears flowed freely down her face at this point, so her mouth tasted like smoke-and-tequila-flavored salt water. My arms circled her back, her hands warmed my face, and we kissed.

After a few seconds, she pulled away from me. "Take off your clothes."

I sat up and started to pull my pants down. I had got-ten one leg out when I froze.

"What's wrong?" Madeline had already made it out of

195

her shorts. Her black lace panties hugged her hips like they had been painted on.

My legs jiggled as I stood and stumbled backward. "I think I'm officially trashed," I said. And the last thing I remembered was the red-carpeted floor rushing up to meet me as I fell.

chapter 17

I woke up to the sound of groaning—a deep, unearthly noise that resonated throughout the room. As I struggled to open my eyes, I realized it was coming from me.

My head rested on a pillow, but I wasn't on the bed. My mattress consisted of the frayed red carpet and dust bunnies. A blanket half covered my shirtless chest.

I sat up, and immediately fell back down. Sunlight flooded the room, bashing into my face with the force of a lead pipe. It hurt to even breathe.

I held my hand to my face in order to block the glare. From above me, I could see Madeline's foot hanging over the edge of the bed.

"Are you awake?" I whispered.

Silence.

I reached up and tapped her big toe. "Madeline?"

Her foot sluggishly moved. "What do you want?"

"I don't feel so good. I think I'm going to be sick."

Madeline reached over the edge of the bed and swiped her hand through the air until it connected with a small plastic trash can. She picked it up and flung it toward me.

"Use that," she said. "And drink some water."

"How am I supposed to get water when I can't even walk?"

"Crawl."

I grabbed the trash can, which had barely reached me, and started crawling. After an eternity, I reached the bathroom. The cold linoleum felt refreshing against my warm palms.

I grabbed the sink and pulled myself up. Immediately, the taste of disgust hit the back of my throat. I quickly turned, flipped up the toilet seat, and threw up.

After finishing up with a few dry heaves, I flushed and returned to the sink. I rinsed my mouth out and forced myself to drink as much water as I could.

Not quite crawling, but not quite walking either, I made it out of the bathroom. Madeline, clad in an oversized T-shirt, was sprawled facedown across the bed. I would have stayed for a while at the base of the bed to stare at her legs, but my own legs wouldn't cooperate.

I collapsed back into my homemade mattress. "I threw up." After waiting a few seconds for a response, I nudged her foot. "Did you hear me? I threw up."

The bed creaked as she moved. "You use the trash can?"

"No. The toilet."

"Good. Now go to sleep," she mumbled. "You'll feel bet-ter once you wake back up."

"Promise?"

I was answered by the sound of her snoring.

*　*　*

When I woke up again, the room was much darker, on account of the shades being drawn. The beating in my head had slowed to a steady, monotonous thud.

"Ready to get up yet?" Madeline asked. She wasn't be-side me, but it still sounded like she was screaming into my ear.

"No."

"Get up anyway. You need to call your parents."

I sat up. She was sitting up in bed, still wearing the same huge T-shirt. She had tucked her entire body un-derneath the shirt so that nothing but her head, neck, and toes were exposed.

"What time is it?" I asked, trying to keep my head steady. I'd quickly discovered that any head movements I made, even minor ones, were greeted with an ungodly amount of pain.

"A little after noon." She pointed at my phone, which was lighting up like the annual church Nativity scene. "It's been like that all morning."

I grabbed the phone. Twelve missed calls.

I started to speed-dial my parents, but I knew I wasn't in any condition to speak to them. Instead, I called Tony.

"Joshua, where the hell are you?"

I held the phone a little farther away from my ear. "I'm sorry. I should have called last night, but I was preoccupied."

There was a long pause on the other end of the phone. "You're with Madeline, aren't you?"

"Tony, I need you to call my parents. Tell them I'm okay, and that I'll call them this evening."

"Josh . . ."

"I'll fill you in later. Call my parents, okay?" Before Tony could argue, I hung up and turned off my phone.

"So what happened last night?" I asked.

"You got drunk." She untucked her legs from out of her T-shirt. Briefly, I saw a flash of black lace. "I ordered us some sandwiches. You need to eat." She walked to the table. "You'll feel better after you get something in your stomach."

The events of that morning flooded back into my head. "I don't know if I should eat. I threw up this morning."

"And last night."

I stood and looked down at my chest, then searched the floor. "Where's my shirt?"

"I tossed it in the Dumpster last night. You threw up all over it." She grabbed a Styrofoam container and sat on the bed. "What the hell did you eat for lunch, by the way?"

"I didn't eat lunch. I was too busy looking for you."

Madeline bowed her head and whispered a few words under her breath. There was still a slight trace of purple on her lips. After she finished praying, she looked at me. "First rule of drinking: Don't get wasted on an empty stomach."

I grabbed my food and sat down at the desk. I mumbled a quick blessing, and opened my eyes to see Madeline staring at me.

"Do you have a standard prayer that you say when you bless your food?" she asked.

"I used to. But lately, I've found that I pray for random things. Like just now, after thanking God for providing this food, I also asked him to look after my parents, to help them not to worry about me." I picked up a french fry and took a nibble of it. "I also thanked him for helping me find you."

Madeline fingered her necklace. "Funny. I thanked him for the same thing."

We munched on our food in silence, pausing every few bites to flash timid smiles at each other. It was nice being there with her, without words.

"You're pretty quiet over there," she said. "Maybe your tongue finally got tired after all the talking you did last night. You were quite the chatterbox."

I didn't like the way she was grinning. "What did I say?"

"I think your exact words were, 'You have the most beautiful, grandiose, gargantuan breasts I have ever seen.'" She smiled even wider. "Then you squeezed my nipple."

"Good Lord." I turned away from her. "Please don't tell me anything else. I don't think I can take it."

"Don't worry, that was as bad as it got. We kissed a little, but you fell asleep before anything else could happen." She paused to take a sip of water. "But that was probably for the best. Take it from me—drunk sex sucks."

I wanted to nod, but I wasn't so sure I agreed with her. Of course, I wasn't sure if I disagreed with her, either.

I glanced at the lumpy pillow on the floor. "How did I end up down there?"

"That's where we happened to be when you fell asleep. And as much as I like you, I was *not* going to sleep on the floor with you." She brushed her bangs to the side of her face. "I was a little jealous—you were out like a log. I bet you could have slept through an earthquake."

I took another bite of my ham and cheese sandwich. It tasted like cardboard. "You didn't sleep well?"

She shook her head. "I eventually fell asleep around eight o'clock this morning. But, if I'd known you were going to wake me up twenty minutes later, I would have stayed up and finished my book."

"You read last night?"

She nodded. "I have a really hard time going to sleep at night. Too many thoughts—too many memories keep running through my head." She glanced at the bottle of tequila. "It used to be that a few shots would put me out, but that doesn't even seem to work anymore."

I put my sandwich down. "Madeline. Last night . . . what you said about you and the preacher—"

"Don't start, Joshua. I'm not in the mood." She started eating again. "As soon as I finish my sandwich, I'm going to take a shower. After I get out, you should do the same. Then I think you'd better go home."

"Like this? Are you crazy?"

"All you did was get drunk and stay out all night.

It sounds bad, but believe me, it could have been a lot worse."

I stared at Madeline, but she was too preoccupied with her sandwich to look back at me. She wore basically nothing, and she looked more beautiful than ever. Not necessarily sexy, but lavishly beautiful.

"Are you still leaving town?" I asked.

"As soon as I can cash my check." She glanced at her watch. "Being that it's so late, it'll probably be tomorrow before I leave."

"You want me to take you by the coffee shop?"

"Sure. But no questions about me and the preacher, okay?"

I nodded, and my head screamed in pain.

* * *

I watched Madeline race across the street, her large purse flapping against her side. We were at our second stop, the bank. She had changed into her usual fare: a tank top, shorts, and flip-flops. I was wearing recycled underwear and jeans, and according to the label on my shirt, my name was Frank and I worked at Lindsey's Brake Repair.

Once Madeline disappeared into the building, I flipped open my cell phone and made a call.

"Joshua?" Dad answered. He sounded like he hadn't slept in a week.

"It's me," I said. "I'm sorry for not calling sooner."

"Hold on a second." I heard him mumble something far away from the receiver. "Your mother's going to get on the line as well."

"I don't want to talk to her."

"You're not in a position to make any demands," he said. A few seconds later, Mom picked up the phone.

"Joshua, baby? Are you okay? Is everything all right?"

"I'm okay." I nodded, as though that would validate my words. "Did Tony call?"

"He just left a few minutes ago," Dad said. "He told us you were with Madeline."

"Joshua, is this because of what I did?" Mom's voice shook. "I'm so sorry, I didn't mean—"

"Mom, it's not because of that." I was still mad at her, but it tore me up inside to hear her pleading with me. "I'm trying to convince Madeline to stay in town."

"She's not going back to Virginia?" Dad asked.

"She refuses to go back, and I don't blame her." I took a deep breath. "That's why I'm calling. I need a big favor. Can Madeline stay with us for a while?"

"I don't know," Dad said. "Maybe your mother and I should talk about this first."

"There's not enough time for that. I'm pretty sure I can stop her from running off, but only if she has someplace to stay."

"Joshua, I'm sorry," Mom said. "I just don't trust her."

"You don't have to trust *her*. Trust me." I closed my eyes. "Proverbs, chapter one, verse eight."

At first I thought my folks had hung up, they were so quiet. Finally, Dad spoke. "'Listen, my son, to your father's instruction and do not forsake your mother's teaching.'"

"You guys have taught me everything I know." My

hand was sweaty against the phone. "Please. Help me. I know I'm doing the right thing."

"Joshua . . ." Mom's voice was faltering.

"I admit, she's made mistakes. But it's not our place to judge her. 'Let he who is without sin cast the first stone.'"

"Are you going to quote every verse in the Bible?" Mom asked.

"Yes, if that's what it takes."

Dad sighed. "Lily, he's a good kid. And more importantly, he's right."

Mom didn't reply, but I could hear her breaths. They were quick and shallow, the total opposite of Dad's.

"Hold on for a minute, Joshua," Mom said. "Your father and I need to talk."

"But—"

"We'll be back in a second," she said. "Just hold on."

I heard some mumbling, but I couldn't make out any words. I glanced at the bank. Madeline had made it to a teller.

A voice got louder on the other end of the phone. "Joshua, this is your mother. I asked Isaiah to hang up so we could talk privately. I just need to talk to my son—my baby—without you or your father trying to quote every damn verse in the Bible."

My mouth dropped open. Mom had cursed.

"Now look," she continued. "I'm sorry for saying all those things about Madeline to her father. When I told you to stop seeing her, it wasn't because I thought she was a bad person. I was just trying to protect you."

"I don't need protection."

"Yes, you do, whether you realize it or not. You're like your father—stubborn and righteous, filled with the belief that you can save anyone. The problem is, unlike your father, you're a seventeen-year-old kid." She sighed. "I don't trust Madeline, Joshua, but I trust you. So if you say she needs help, we'll help her."

I wished more than anything that I was with Mom at that point. I had never wanted to hug her so badly. "I'm going to need a little more time to convince her to stay. I probably won't be home until tomorrow."

"Tomorrow!"

I peered at the bank again. Madeline was stuffing something into her purse and heading toward the car. "Mom, trust me, okay?"

"You've got one more day," she said. "Tomorrow afternoon, your butt better be back in this house, or I swear, God Himself won't be able to save you."

"Thanks, Mom." I scooted lower in the seat so Madeline couldn't see me on the phone. "I'd better get off—"

"Wait," Mom said. "I don't want any details of where y'all are staying or what you're doing. I just want you to promise me you'll be . . . responsible."

My face flashed hot. "Mom, we haven't—we're not going to—"

"Promise me."

I huffed. "I'll be safe. I promise. Now I really need to get off the phone. I love you guys. Bye."

Just as I was putting the phone back into my pocket,

Madeline opened the passenger-side door. "Everything work out okay?" I asked.

She nodded, although she didn't look at me. "No problems at all. Since Dad's listed on my account, I figured he would try to put a hold on my checking account and credit cards, but I don't think he even tried." She slumped into her seat. "It's like he's begging me to run off."

I started up the car, then grabbed her hand. "You hungry?"

She shook her head, still staring into space.

"Maybe we should stop by the nursing home," I said. "You could say good-bye to the old-timers."

Madeline didn't reply. I took her silence as affirmation, and headed down the street.

* * *

As soon as we entered the rec room, Ms. Beatrice waved to us. "You'll never guess what happened," she said. "Rollins beat Leonard at chess."

"Damn straight," Mr. Rollins said. He was almost doubled over in his wheelchair, although he raised his head slightly to look at us. Well, to look at Madeline. "It took me five years, but I finally beat him." His voice was barely above a whisper.

"Yeah, you got me," Leonard chimed in. "Now, why don't you calm down a little. You know you ain't supposed to be getting all excited."

Ms. Beatrice fanned her hand at Mr. Rollins. "Come on, Carl. You've had enough fun. Why don't you lie down for a spell?"

Mr. Rollins had lost a few pounds since the last time I saw him; his skin flapped loosely underneath his jaw. He narrowed his eyes at Ms. Beatrice. "Last time I checked, you weren't my wife."

She placed her hands on her hips. "Since when has that stopped me from bossing you around."

Mr. Rollins's rebuttal was offset by a violent coughing attack. He hunched over even farther, his knees pushing into his chest.

The scowl on Ms. Beatrice's face melted away. "Oh, Carl . . ."

Mr. Rollins finally stopped coughing. "Perhaps I'll lie down, just for a little bit."

Madeline placed her hand on the back of his wheelchair. "Why don't I walk back with you?"

Mr. Rollins smiled, displaying the huge gap between his front teeth. "I knew there was a reason I liked you so much."

"Come on, honey," Ms. Beatrice said to Madeline. "I'll walk with you."

Once Madeline wheeled Mr. Rollins away, Leonard turned to me. "He sho' looked happy, didn't he?"

I nodded and sat down at the table. "I can't believe he finally won."

Leonard motioned for me to move closer. "I let him win," he whispered. "You think after all these years I was gonna forget about his rook sitting in the corner of the board? I may be getting senile, but I ain't *that* crazy."

"He's really sick, isn't he?"

Leonard nodded. "I figured for once, he should win at somethin'." He fiddled with one of the remaining pawns on the board. "Rollins has been fighting his whole life. I think that's 'bout the only thing he's good at. Sometimes he wins and sometimes he loses, but he keeps fightin'."

"That was very noble of you." I picked up one of the pieces. "You want to play a quick game?"

His eyes crinkled. "I didn't know you played chess."

"Well, I've never actually played before." I began placing the pieces back on the board. "But I've watched you and Mr. Rollins enough to get the general rules of the game."

Leonard helped me finish setting up the board. "I really appreciate you playing with me. I just hope you don't get as mad as Rollins does when I whup him."

"Maybe I'll surprise you and win."

"Maybe." He slid the last piece into place. "But probably not."

*   *   *

After Leonard very thoroughly and very quickly beat me at two chess games, I got up to find Madeline.

I stopped by Ms. Beatrice's room first. She was leaning back in her recliner, watching a sitcom.

"Joshua, you still here?" She grabbed her remote and muted the television. "I figured you'd left by now."

"I was waiting for Madeline. She hasn't made it back to the rec room yet."

"Lord, she must still be talking to Carl. He's been telling *everyone* his life story." She snorted. "Like someone cares 'bout that old fool."

From across the room, I could see that Ms. Beatrice's eyes were getting moist. "Leonard said he wasn't doing well."

"He don't have much time left." She sat up in her chair. "Your daddy dropped by here looking for you, you know."

"I'm not surprised. I talked to him before I came by."

"He called and told us he had gotten hold of you. He didn't explain what was going on, but I figured it had somethin' to do with Maddie."

"She's planning to run off. I'm trying to stop her." I shook my head. "I'm *going* to stop her."

"You're gonna have a tough time with that, you know. My little Maddie can be pretty darn stubborn." She smiled. "But if anyone can talk any sense into her, you can. Just don't be so eager to save her that you lose yourself."

I stiffened. "I know what I'm doing."

"I'm sure you think you do." She picked up the remote. "You better go rescue Maddie. Ain't no telling what Carl's said to her by now."

I closed Ms. Beatrice's door behind me and continued down the hallway. Before I even reached Mr. Rollins's room, I heard his voice filling the corridor. I entered the room to see him and Madeline doubled over in laughter.

Madeline wiped her eyes. "I'm sorry, Joshua. I was about to head back."

"No problem. It gave Leonard and me some time to play a couple of games of chess." I moved closer to Mr. Rollins. "I thought you were supposed to be in bed."

Madeline laughed again. "I've already tried to get him

into bed, and both times, he waved me off. It seems Mr. Rollins has had a miraculous recovery since leaving the recreation room."

Mr. Rollins's eyes had more of a spark in them. "Leonard told you he let me win, didn't he?"

I shifted my gaze to the door. "I don't know what you're talking about," I mumbled.

"Boy, you the worst liar I ever met," he said. "I'm sick, and most days I can't even take two breaths before coughing, but today ain't one of them days." He winked at Madeline. "I ain't felt this good in two weeks."

"But all that moaning and coughing?" I asked.

"I was fakin'."

I snapped my fingers. "You knew he was going to throw the game. You knew he was going to let you win."

"Like my daddy used to say, if you can't win, cheat." Then he picked up Madeline's hand and pecked it. "Ms. Madeline, thank you for gracing me with your presence once again. It's always a pleasure."

Madeline stood and did a half curtsy. "The pleasure is all mine," she replied with a thick Southern accent. She walked to the door, but paused before exiting the room. "You take care of yourself."

He nodded. "And you do the same."

I waved good-bye to Mr. Rollins, and we headed to the car. I was surprised when Madeline slipped her arm into mine.

"Mr. Rollins told me that your dad came by looking for you."

I nodded. "I talked to him while you were in the bank."

"Is he mad?"

"Yeah, but not as mad as I thought he'd be."

She stopped walking. "Why didn't you tell me you were supposed to be going to Savannah for a youth retreat?"

I laughed. "I must have been too busy drinking and throwing up."

"That's not funny, Joshua." She unlinked her arm. "The more you hang around me, the more fucked up your life gets, and all you can do is make jokes?"

"You're not . . . *ruining* my life," I said. "I've been to Savannah plenty of times. There's nothing there I haven't seen before."

"But Joshua—"

"The fact of the matter is, I'm not supposed to be there. I'm supposed to be here. With you."

"I bet your father thinks otherwise."

"You know, it really doesn't matter what my father thinks." I took her hand and intertwined her fingers with mine. "It doesn't matter what your father thinks, either."

Madeline spent the next few seconds focusing on a passing car.

"You can stay with us if you want to." I lightly squeezed her hand.

The sun had sunk close to the horizon, casting Madeline's face in a yellow glow. "Yeah, like your folks really want me crashing at your house." As she let out a little spurt of laughter, her bottom lip trembled.

"I asked them, and they said yes. The guest room is all yours if you want it."

She swallowed hard. "I used to wonder how I would have turned out if I had had parents like yours. Good parents. Parents who cared . . ." Her voice cracked. "Parents who actually listened to me."

I thought back to my phone conversation with my parents. Madeline was right—they *were* good parents. By no means were they perfect, but when it counted—when it mattered most—they trusted me. They believed in me. They listened to me.

"Well, what do you say?" I asked. "Will you come home with me?"

"Joshua, I can't. . . ." She cleared her throat, then took a deep breath. "I'm leaving. I've made up my mind."

I could have said more, but I didn't want to push her. Not yet. "I just wanted to offer."

"You've done due diligence." She pulled away from me and headed to the car. "Consider yourself off the hook."

chapter 18

Madeline stuffed the last article of clothing into her bag and zipped it shut. "I think that's everything."

In what could only be classified as a modern-day miracle, Madeline was able to force all her clothes, shoes, and books into her two bags, with the clothes she planned to wear tomorrow draped over the back of the wooden chair. Looking at the motel room now, you would never guess that this was the same room we had slept in last night.

Madeline had taken a shower and changed back into her oversized T-shirt. For the first time since she had been back to Conway, I couldn't see any hint of purple on her body. No lipstick. No nail polish. Nothing.

The air in the room seemed to be charged. Every time

I looked at Madeline, walking around in nothing but that T-shirt, all I could think about was what we almost did last night. What I wished we had done. What I still wanted to do—I think.

I looked at the bottle of tequila standing solitary on the desk. "Not taking that with you?"

"I figured I'd leave it for you."

"There's no way I'm touching that stuff again. I still can't feel my fingers."

She placed her hand on the neck of the bottle. "Too bad. It was fun drinking with you. Much better than drinking alone."

"Yeah, and other than the mind-wrenching headache, excessive vomiting, and skin-peeling slap you gave me, it was the best time of my life." I scooted to the edge of the bed. "Why *did* you slap me, by the way?"

"The way you sounded, so adamant and so righteous, you reminded me of my dad."

"Well then, why did you kiss me?"

"Because you're *not* my dad." She dropped the bottle into the trash, then sat beside me. "I don't think he's spoken a kind word to me in four years."

"Your dad was wrong," I said. "None of this was your fault."

"Maybe. Maybe not. It doesn't really matter anymore."

"It matters to me." I took her hand. "Don't go."

"Joshua, you don't understand. I need a place where I can blend in. Where no one knows me. Where I can disappear."

It felt like Madeline was trying to pull away from me,

but I refused to release her hand. I could feel her cracking—I knew she was close to changing her mind. I just needed a little more time. "Please, stay. I won't judge you." I paused. "I'll even let you slap me again, if that helps."

"I think you've had enough abuse." She smiled and squeezed my hand, her skin soft against mine. "Are you sure you're not going home tonight?"

"Not unless you're kicking me out."

She looked at the back of my hand. "I'm not kicking you out," she whispered. Then she yawned.

"Ready for bed?"

She nodded. "I have a lot of traveling to do tomorrow."

Madeline still hadn't told me where she was planning to go. Whenever I asked, all she would say was *far away*.

We sat there for a few more minutes, her rubbing my hand, me trying to come up with something interesting to say. Then she yawned again, and then I yawned, and then we laughed a little.

Finally, I caved. I grabbed one of the pillows and threw it onto the floor. "Be sure not to step on me in the middle of the night."

She glanced at the two remaining pillows on the bed. "Is that what you want? To sleep on the floor?"

"I don't. It's just— "

"Joshua." She kissed the back of my hand. "I want you to come to bed. With me."

I stared at her for a long time—so long that I almost lost myself in her gaze. And as much as I wanted to be thinking about her, I found myself thinking about everything *but* her.

The church said that premarital sex was wrong.

Jenn believed it was okay if you were in love.

Tony said that we were young; we had the rest of our lives to "live right."

And I . . . I didn't know *what* I believed.

But I did know this: I loved Madeline Smith. Even after all these years, she was my best friend. She knew me better than anyone else. She understood me better than anyone else.

And I knew I wanted her—wanted *this*—more than anything else I had ever wanted.

Maybe it was wrong, wanting to be with her. But if it really was a sin, it was one I could live with.

"Joshua?" She let go of my hand. "It's okay. We don't have to if you don't want to. I just thought . . . I'm sorry."

"No," I whispered. "I want to. I'm sure."

She smiled. "Then go turn off the lights."

As she scampered into bed, I checked to make sure the door was locked and turned off the lights. Moonlight spilled through the window, illuminating my path back to the bed.

"Hurry up," she said. "It's cold under these sheets."

I kicked off my shoes and slipped underneath the covers. I knew I should have probably taken off my shirt—well, Frank's shirt—and my jeans, but with the way my lower extremities were acting, the more layers I could keep between me and Madeline, the better.

I lay in the bed, my body stiff, my mind racing. I mean, it was about to happen. It was really about to happen!

Madeline put her hand against my chest. "Good Lord,

Joshua, your heart feels like it's about to burst," she said. "Calm down, baby. Everything's going to be all right."

Baby? The only other person who had ever called me baby was my mother.

It sounded so much better coming from Madeline.

"What about . . ." I gulped. "What about condoms?"

"In the top drawer of your nightstand. I put them there earlier tonight."

"Oh. Good. Now all I have to do is figure out how to put one on."

"Don't worry. We'll take things as slow as you want." She kissed the bottom of my chin before yawning once more. "We could just go to sleep, too. That wouldn't be so bad."

With the way my body was revved up, there was no way I was going to sleep anytime soon.

I took a deep breath, and then, straining my neck as much as humanly possible, I kissed her, very lightly at first. And then those very light kisses turned into heavy, body-shaking, soul-stirring kisses. She kicked the sheets from her legs and pressed her bare feet against mine. They were cool, but not cold.

At some point, the kissing became more than kissing as my fingers traced a path from her jawline to her neck to the valley between her breasts. It was the thinnest of material that separated my skin from hers.

I slid my hands to her hips. My fingertips brushed against her underwear, and I immediately jerked my hands back to the safety of her cotton T-shirt.

Madeline stopped kissing me for long enough to climb

on top of me, and then guided my hands back to her hips. "You can take off my T-shirt if you want to."

I nodded and cupped my fingers underneath the edges of her shirt as she brought her hands over her head. I peeled the shirt away from her body, and reveled in her nakedness.

She looked down at her breasts. "They're too big," she said.

"They're beautiful." I ran my fingers across her stomach. "You're beautiful."

"No offense, but you're probably not the most objective person at this point." Then she laughed and covered her chest, like she suddenly realized she was naked. "You know, I've never understood the fascination that guys have with breasts. When you think about it, it's nothing but skin and fat."

"Um . . . I don't know. I've never really thought about it like that before. . . ."

She frowned. "I'm sorry for babbling on like this. The last thing you want to hear right now is how much I hate my breasts." She started kissing me again. "I promise, no more interruptions."

"No, it's okay," I mumbled, my mouth half-covered with hers. "Tell me what else you don't like."

She leaned back. "Are you serious? You really want to know?"

I pulled her to me; she nestled into my arms like she was made to fit there. "Of course. I could use all the help I can get. This is uncharted territory for me."

She laughed, and before I knew it, I was laughing as well. And things just seemed so much . . . easier all of a sudden.

"Nipples," she said. "I hate it when guys squeeze my nipples. It's like they're trying to tear them off." She reached under my shirt and tweaked one of my nipples. "Really, does that feel good?"

I flinched as she dug her fingernails into me. "No, I suppose not."

"See, I think every guy should get their nipples squeezed, just to see how uncomfortable it is." She spoke into my neck, each word a cool breeze on my sticky skin. "So what about you? There's got to be something girls do that you hate."

I chewed on my lip for a second. "Well, there was this one time when Jenn stuck her tongue in my ear. . . ."

And that was how it went. We bounced from talking about what we didn't like about making out to what foods we didn't like, to what we didn't like about our families, to everything.

We would stop talking every few minutes to kiss and grope and twist around in the sheets, but we somehow always got back to talking again. As much as I wanted her body, I wanted to talk to her more.

And with the way Madeline kept laughing and smiling, I knew she felt the same way.

It wasn't until I was halfway into my story about one of our basketball games that I noticed her slow breathing. I paused and listened. Her entire body seemed to sigh with each deep breath.

"Madeline?"

She responded by snuggling against me. Her breaths hit the tip of my nose, making me want to sneeze. Her elbow jutted into my side.

"Madeline?" I repeated. "Are you asleep?"

"Um . . ." Her eyelids moved but didn't open. "I'm awake. We still . . . have to . . ."

Then she started snoring.

I chuckled. This was not what I had in mind when I climbed into bed with her.

I wanted to wake her. I mean, I *really* wanted to wake her. A slight nudge was all it would take.

It would have been easy. So easy.

She wouldn't have even been upset. She probably never expected the night to end like this, either.

But I couldn't do it. I just couldn't do it.

Not because I was a preacher's son. Not because my parents wouldn't have approved. Not because the Bible said it was wrong.

I let her sleep because she was my friend, I loved her, and she deserved to have one good night of rest.

So I stared at the ceiling, trying my best not to be miserable while Madeline snored beside me. My back hurt, my neck hurt . . . my entire body hurt.

But I didn't move for the rest of the night. And Madeline slept like a baby.

* * *

I woke up the next morning in an empty bed. I jumped up from the mattress, the blood thundering in my ears. Then I saw her two overstuffed bags leaning against the wall.

I sighed. *She was still here.*

Once I realized Madeline hadn't run off in the middle of the night, my body remembered how tired it was. It had been well after four o'clock when I finally fell asleep.

I thought about going back to sleep, but instead I decided to take a shower, in the hope that that would wake me up. By the time I got out, Madeline had returned. She wore a yellow T-shirt that reminded me of lemonade and sunshine. And like last night, she was without makeup.

"Sorry I was gone for so long." She held up a paper bag and a Styrofoam cup. "To make up for it, I got us some doughnuts and coffee." She took a sip from the cup. "I think we've kissed enough to make it okay for us to share a cup of coffee."

"Thanks." I sat down beside her. "I didn't hear you get up this morning."

"I tread lightly."

My fingers brushed against hers as I took the dough-nuts. I reached into the bag and started to grab the plain one, but picked chocolate-covered instead.

"I'm glad you took the chocolate one," she said as she fished out the remaining doughnut. "I'm trying to watch my weight, remember."

"And like I said before, you're perfect like you are." I licked my chocolate-smudged fingertips. "Where did you go, by the way? Just to get breakfast?"

"To pay for the room." She took a bite of her doughnut and chewed slowly. "And to go see my aunt." With her free hand, she reached into her purse and pulled out my keys. "Thanks for letting me borrow your car, by the way."

"Um . . . you're welcome?" I gulped down some coffee while she swallowed the last of her doughnut. "What did you and your aunt talk about?"

"I needed some information," she said. "It took a few hours, but she finally gave me what I was looking for. It's not much, but it's a name, a number, and an address. More than I ever had before."

I thought for a few minutes, the coffee warm and soothing in my stomach. "Your birth mother?"

Madeline nodded. "I always had the feeling Aunt Gwen knew who she was, but would never tell me," she said. "She lives in Texas now. I've decided I want to meet her—face to face."

Fear clutched at my throat. "You're going to Texas!" I jumped from the bed and in the process spilled coffee on the floor. "You've never even met the woman before!"

"Joshua, she's my mother. I want to know her." She nodded toward the phone. "While you were in the shower, I called Greyhound and bought my ticket. My bus leaves at a quarter after ten."

I glanced at my watch. "But that's in an hour! That's too soon!"

"It's the only bus leaving today," she said, her voice calm. "Plus, I have to catch the bus in Myrtle Beach. Conway's too small to have a terminal."

I looked into her eyes, hoping to see the slightest hint of hesitation. Of worry. Of self-doubt.

Unfortunately, all I saw was resolve.

"You're really going, aren't you?" I collapsed back into the bed. "I guess I always thought . . . I just figured . . ." I turned away from her. I didn't want her to see the tears collecting in my eyes.

This was all wrong! She wasn't supposed to be going. She wasn't supposed to be running away. I was supposed to stop her.

I was supposed to save her.

"Joshua? Please, say something."

"What do you want me to say? That I'm happy?"

"Actually, that's exactly what I had hoped you'd say." She patted my thigh. "I'm going to meet my mother. My *real* mother."

I scooted farther away from her. "Your real mother lives in Virginia."

She didn't respond. It took a second, but I finally realized she was crying. I turned around to see her fighting back tears. Like me.

"I talked to Mom this morning. I'm not . . . welcome there anymore. Dad decided it was best if I stay away." She sniffed. "Apparently, I'm not worth saving."

I took her hand, wet from where her tears had splashed against her skin. "Don't listen to your father. He's a–"

"Dick. Jackass. Bastard." She shrugged. "But he's also right. I don't belong there."

"Then stay here!" I could hear the desperation pouring out of my voice. "What about your aunt? She'll be worried sick if you leave," I said, but what I was really thinking was: What about me?

"She'll be okay." She touched my cheek. "Please. Just be happy for me."

I wanted to smile for her, I really did. But my body was too busy trying to stop my heart from cracking in two.

* * *

Even though Myrtle Beach was about a half hour away from Conway, the drive to the Greyhound terminal seemed to pass instantaneously. I had prayed for a flood, a swarm of locusts, anything to slow us down, but we weren't so lucky.

"You don't have to wait," she said as I pulled into the terminal. "If you want, you can drop me off."

I was already heading to the parking lot. "I'm going in with you."

For once, she didn't argue.

We parked and I popped open the trunk. She grabbed one bag, I grabbed the other, and we headed to the terminal. Hundreds of reasons for her to stay jumped into my head, but no words made it past my lips.

Once inside the building, she dropped her bag beside a bench. "Wait here. I'll be back in a second."

I watched Madeline march toward the ticket booth. She seemed to be swallowed up by the sheer emptiness of the room. After spending a few minutes talking to a woman behind the counter, Madeline reached into her purse and pulled out her wallet.

I wondered how long her trip would take. I wondered if my parents would ever forgive me if I went with her.

I felt like I should run across the room, fling my arms

around her, and ask her to stay. Not ask. *Beg. Plead.* She couldn't go. I wanted her. I *needed* her. And she needed me.

I swear, I almost did run across that room, but by the time I had made up my mind to do it, Madeline was walking back toward me. "The bus should be boarding in a few minutes." She took my hand and pulled me onto the bench with her. Her fingers drummed a steady beat on the back of my hand.

"Nervous?" I asked.

"Is it that noticeable?" She laughed. "Yeah, I'm nervous. Scared, even. But not about the trip." She squeezed my hand. "I need to ask you something. And I need you to be honest with me. Okay?"

I nodded, unable to read Madeline's expression. "Okay."

She took a deep breath. "Last night . . . why didn't you wake me up? Did I do something wrong?"

I quickly shook my head. "No. Of course not. You were perfect."

"Then what was it?" She looked toward the ticket booth, away from me. "What made you change your mind? Do you find me . . . I don't know. Dirty? Tainted?"

"You know I could never think anything like that about you." I released her hand and turned her so that we were facing each other. "I wanted to wake you, but I know how hard it is for you to go to sleep. And you just looked so peaceful." I smiled. "I guess as much as I wanted to have sex, you seemed like you needed sleep more."

Madeline stared at me as her eyes grew moist. Finally, she placed her hand on my cheek and kissed me softly on the lips. "You really are one of the good guys, Joshua Wynn."

"And so are you," I whispered back.

Madeline wrapped her arms around my neck and hugged me tightly, rubbing her wet cheek against my dry skin. "You smell nice," she said after a minute. "Is that cologne?"

"It must be your shampoo. I used it this morning."

"Really?" She sniffed above my ear. "Funny, it smells different on you than it does on me." Then Madeline pulled away from me. "I've been waiting for the right time to give you something, but I guess it's either now or never." She reached into her backpack, and after fumbling around in it for a few moments, she pulled out a spiral-bound notebook.

"I kept my promise. I wrote to you, just like I said I would." She placed the notebook in my lap and flipped it open. "I just never got around to mailing any of the letters."

I ran my fingers across the page. "This whole notebook is full of letters to me?"

She nodded. "It's a mix of letters and poems." She closed the notebook. "I want you to have it."

"No, I can't–"

"I wrote them for you." She smiled. "I always knew I'd give them to you. This way, I get to save on postage."

I stared at the cover of the notebook for a few seconds,

then flipped it back open. Her words, of course, were penned in purple ink.

She placed her hand over the page. "Save it for later. After I'm gone."

I nodded. "Is this supposed to keep me warm in the middle of the night?"

She laughed, but stopped when the intercom announced the final boarding of her bus.

We both stood, but neither of us made a move toward the door.

She shrugged. "Well, I guess I should—"

I pulled her to me, stifling her words, not wanting to let her go. The scent of vanilla and coffee filled my soul once again, but this time, I couldn't tell if the smell came from her or from me.

Her hands settled at the base of my neck. "Thank you," she whispered into my ear. "Thank you for giving a damn about me. Thank you for . . . trying."

I pulled back, but just a little, and tried to take a snapshot of this girl in the yellow T-shirt, her face full of freckles and pain and beauty and laughter. Then I kissed her again.

And again. And again.

As she slipped her hands under my shirt, her palms red-hot against my cool back, I realized that I had no idea what the next hour would lead to. And I surely had no idea what the next few days, weeks, and months would lead to.

All I knew was that I had done what I was supposed to do. I had tried.

For Madeline's sake, I prayed that would be enough.

Dear Madeline,

I know I haven't written you in a few weeks, but life's been pretty busy, with school starting back up and everything.

Mom and Dad finally lifted their punishment— I think they just got tired of me hovering around the house all the time. Tony and I got in a game of hoops yesterday, although he spent more time asking about you than focusing on the game. He's convinced that we did "the deed."

My response: A gentleman never tells.

The one good thing about being confined to the house for so long was that I had the chance to read—and reread—all your letters.

Let me tell you, those were not easy reads.

I'm not quite sure I have the capacity to hate someone, but if I do, your father would be at the top of my list. He's the type of person who gives preachers a bad name. Actually, he's the type of person who gives human beings in general a bad name.

But I know you don't like discussing your father, so I won't say anything else on that matter.

The old-timers at the nursing home wanted me to tell you hello. Mr. Rollins is still waiting for a sponge bath you supposedly promised to give him.

The biggest news since my last letter is that I resigned as president of the youth group. I thought Mom and Dad were going to have a fit when I told them, but they were pretty cool about it. I think they understand that I'm trying to figure some things out, and I just can't do it while being the head of the group.

That being said, according to Rachel, half the members have dropped out since Donna took over as president. Last Sunday, Mrs. Anderson cornered me in the sanctuary and strongly encouraged me to start coming back to meetings. I declined.

Speaking of church, guess who was there last Sunday? Your aunt! We talked for a bit after service. Of course, the conversation was mainly about you.

You're quite a hard person to get ahold of, you know. Your aunt tried to call you a few times, but your mom's phone is disconnected. And every letter she tried to mail got sent back by the post office.

It did make her feel better to know that I got a postcard from you last week, but like always, you neglected to include a return address. Why is that? Are you worried your aunt or I would hightail it to you as soon as we knew where you were?

Well, if that's what you're thinking, you're right.

I tried to convince her not to worry—that you're a smart girl and you're going to be okay. But I'll be honest—it's really hard not to worry.

But there's nothing I can do about that. All I can do is pray for your well-being and keep *writing letters. And one day—maybe next week or next month or even next year—you'll show back up, and I'll have my own notebook of letters to give to you.*

Because even though I don't know where you are, I can still write letters. I can still keep my promise.

Anyway, this is going to have to be a quick letter, because I'm meeting with Rachel and a bunch of the girls from church about forming a praise-dance team.

If I time it right, I should have a few extra minutes to grab a cup of coffee on the way.

—Joshua

varian johnson was born and raised in Florence, South Carolina, but now makes his home in Austin, Texas, with his wife and their two cocker spaniels. He is a graduate of the Vermont College of Fine Arts MFA Program for Writing for Children and Young Adults and is the author of *My Life as a Rhombus*. Visit him online at www.varianjohnson.com.